What's Next

BOBBY BELL

ISBN   978-1-64552-039-9   (Paperback)
ISBN   978-1-64552-040-5   (Digital)

Lettra Press books may be ordered through booksellers or by contacting:

Lettra Press LLC
18229 E 52nd Ave.
Denver City, CO 80249
1 303 586 1431 | info@lettrapress.com
www.lettrapress.com

Chapter 1

Seven-year-old Anthony Gallagher holding his brother's, Dennis Gallagher's hand looked up into his brother's blue eyes, "Denny do you see that man over there by the tunnel?"

"You mean the guy wearing a suit in this Florida weather?"

"Don't you think its kind a weird? I mean it is hot outside, and he is the only one in a suit."

"Anthony a lot a people wear suits; specially people who work in some kind of business, or maybe lawyers. Heck even you sometimes wear a tie to school."

"Yeah, Denny, but he keeps looking over here."

❧

Deplaning the 747, and as he was exiting the tunnel from the aircraft into the arrival area, Russell had a feeling he was being stared at. Not so much him as the woman and children standing near him. Shaking his head and pondering his arrival. Still he couldn't help feeling, *is it even possible to be a **little** paranoid? I guess no more than it is for a woman to be a little bit pregnant.* Eighteen months in a very inhospitable country. A place where he felt that his presence was not at all welcome, plus it was miserably hot especially during daylight hours. It could get downright cold at night. He really couldn't help looking around. *Is that short dark man in a very expensive suit staring at me? No! He is definitely looking; hell he ain't looking he is staring I really need to talk to someone about this?* Taking a deep breath, letting it out slowly. *Life goes on.* Within minutes his wife will be in his arms and he will be with his kids.

Feeling as if he'd been in his dress blues for at least a week, Russell Gallagher couldn't believe he was actually home; well almost home. Tampa International Airport still looked the same. The air still had the smell of artificial air and a hundred bodies packed in the cabin of the 747. The small attractive woman with auburn hair standing with three children. *No that can't be them. Those kids are way too big, and the auburn hair of the woman is wrong. When I left at this same gate eighteen months ago my wife's Hair came down to her shoulders. I do have three kids, but they couldn't have grown that much. That little red headed girl with locks, and the stuffed pink bunny is standing on her own. When I left little Jackie was crawling and very... She actually would teeter until she found some something to hold onto; an end table, the coffee table or the couch.*

"Rusty, Russ, over here." It was the woman and the boys were pulling away from her and running towards him.

A boy that stood almost up to his chest with dirty blond hair was running up to him. "Daddy! Here over here." The boy behind him was a tow head, his complexion was almost translucent it was so white, and pale blue eyes. When Rusty asked, the doctor said no he wasn't albino; his skin had pigmentation but he had to be very careful in the sun. The doctor said he was healthy. He was a lot bigger than the Anthony he remembered when he left. The little girl with red locks, just stood there hiding behind her mother, with her stuffed bunny in her left hand and two fingers of her right hand in her nose with the thumb in her mouth.

The two boys were huddled around Russell with Anthony holding on to one pant leg, and Dennis holding his hand, the red haired Jacquelyn with thumb still in her mouth held onto her mother's leg ever tighter and then put her arms up to be lifted into her mother's arms. With eyes that appeared the size of saucers, like a painting by Margaret Keane, and the same color as her mother's; he could never figure out the color of Naomi's eyes either; hazel is what some people call them. She was just staring at her dad. Naomi looked back at Russ, motioning for him to follow her. Trying to yell over the noise of the crowd, "What kind of bag are we looking for?"

Sweat running down his nose and his shirt feeling damp, and sticking to his body, "Only on piece of luggage; the same olive drab duffle bag that I left with. I do have a few more things coming but I put them in my hold baggage."

Putting Jackie down, "Jackie you're a big girl. Can you walk beside mommy for a while?"

Russ bent over to pick up Jackie. He didn't think her hazel eyes could get any bigger. Getting even closer to her mother, "Mommy, I don't want that man to hold me."

"Jackie, that's your daddy."

Squeezing into the small elevator Russ looked over at his wife, and pushing his hat back, "That's OK. Jacquelyn was just a little more than a twinkle when I left. We'll get to know one another."

Looking over at the maroon Chevy Caprice, then at the kids and finally at Naomi, "How's the car been running?" putting out his hand for the keys, "Do I get to drive. It has been a long time. The last thing I drove was a 29 passenger bus on the flight line.

"Naomi," pointing to the same small dark man in the very expensive suit. It was a blue suit, he was wearing a pink shirt and red tie, "is it me or have you noticed him staring at us?"

"Russ you just got out of the Mideast. I'm sure he is not looking at us."

Climbing behind the steering wheel, looking over to the right and patting Russell on the shoulder, "Russ I know you like driving this car, but a few things have changed. First I'm not living with the folks. I got a job as a legal aid in St. Pete. The drive from Sarasota to St. Pete was becoming a hassle. So we're renting a place on the north side of St. Pete. I got Denny and Anthony into the Catholic School; it's not that far from the house. Plus I don't have to take the Jackie to Day Care; the school actually has a day care.

Russell started shaking his hands, as if they were on fire and blowing on his fingers. "Sorry about that, but my hands have been falling asleep lately, and my fingers get cold, and then real hot like they're on fire. Sometimes it feels like I've got fire ants on my hands. I'm sure it's nothing; probably a pinched nerve. St. Pauls'?" Naomi shaking her head, "I went there up to the eighth grade. I actually graduated out of the eighth grade. Actually the folks thought I'd be going on to Bishop Berry High School."

"Why didn't you go on to the Catholic High School? Too Tough?"

"No it wasn't too tough. It was girls. Kinda missed looking at them. Bishop Berry was an all-boys school back then.

Looking over at Russ with half a grin, "I do hope it's only your hands that are numb." There was quiet in the car even the kids seemed to be unusually quiet. Naomi spoke first, "I'd tell you to go over to the clinic, but if you could wait until you talk to your mom she called yesterday and she wants you to call her as soon as you can. I think there might be something wrong with your dad."

Cresting the high point on the Gandy Bridge, "Did mom say what was wrong?"

"She did say your dad was having some breathing problems and they have him on oxygen. She wanted to tell both of us about your dad."

Rubbing the back of his neck, "That oxygen must put a hell of a crimp on his smoking." With her lips pressed tightly together, "**Rusty**... that is not **even** funny."

Russ just couldn't believe how much Tampa Bay had changed. Coming off the Gandy Bridge Naomi turned left on Ninth Street, and within minutes Naomi called to the back seat "Denny open the gate for mommy? Denny...Dennis! Are you awake?"

"What color is that siding?"

"When we first rented it I thought it was sand brown. The landlord informed me the shingle siding is actually what the landlord called it desert brown."

Placing his hand on Naomi's knee, "only in Florida could you get away with that color. I'd almost forgot about Jalousie Windows. This has got to be the only place in the world with Jalousie Windows." Pushing Naomi's skirt up above her knee, "Naomi I think I can handle the gate." Looking over at Naomi. "I honestly don't know what I want first. Food or climbing into bed and sleeping for twelve hours."

In unison from the back seat, even little Jackie, "We want food."

"Naomi, have you been feeding these kids?"

"Yes Russ I do feed our children. Sometimes I don't eat but my kids always get fed."

"I know they do."

"Rusty you need to call your mom." The three kids were sitting at the kitchen table just staring. Anthony was holding a knife in one fist and a fork in the other. Russ had taken his shoes off, grabbed the phone, "Naomi I can't remember their phone number."

After pulling out her address and handing to Russ she walked into the small kitchen, "Alright guys Daddy is calling his mother so please be quiet. We'll call for pizza."

At that there was an unusually hushed, "Yah."

"Naomi, what is that you have in your hand?"

"Oh! It's a cellular phone. I was told I needed it for work. The law firm is paying for it. I'm surprised you don't know what this is. I know some of the people over there in the desert were using them to call home."

With a raised eyebrow, "Russ you have to be the last person on the face of the earth that doesn't have a cell phone. Hell, homeless people have cell phones."

"Yeah I've seen them, but they always seems too expensive. Some of the guys in my outfit were always running out of minutes."

Looking up at Russ was coming out of the bedroom, "Boy that didn't take long. Did you get a chance to talk to your dad?"

"Yeah. He says it's as if he has a slight case of the flue. He doesn't know why the doc wants him to use that oxygen 24/7. I did ask if he has quit smoking. Says he knows better than to smoke near the oxygen tank. I told him we would come for a visit, but didn't know exactly when."

"My boss knows that I might need a little time off. So I have no problem. What about you?"

"I got thirty days. I might go and see my new boss, just to let my new bosses know what's going on. I suppose I could just tell my sponsor what's going on. I haven't met him yet, but we are already invited over for steaks. Says he'll burn them on the grill."

"Well since you're off anyway, I'll go in tomorrow and let my boss know what's going on."

Rubbing his face, and scratching his head, pulling his wife towards him, "Dad seems to be doing pretty good for now. Mom says that it is hard for her to sleep; she hears that oxygen pumping and his breathing. She says it is worse than listening to his snoring. She got used to his labored breathing, it's when he stops that makes her sit up in bed."

Naomi sitting on Russell's lap, leans her head back, "So what are they doing about it?"

"Would you believe that dad is on a list for a transplant? I didn't even know that they could do that."

"Yeah, that has become quite common."

"I know that there has been a lot of progress in heart transplants, but dad's going to need a lung and heart transplant."

"Well they are in Houston where they have some of the best in that field."

"Yeah, but they are doing it at the VA."

Just then the doorbell rang. Naomi pulling herself up off Russell's lap, "OK kids, pizza is here."

It seemed to Russell that the kids were on speed. They were literally bouncing off the walls. "Naomi! "Where is the turn off switch on these kids?"

Sounding like a Marine Drill Instructor Naomi's voice was not quite a deep as a Marines', at least the Marines Russ knew, "**Alright! Let's bring it down.** Now all of you change into sleeping clothes, brush your teeth and come out her when your done so you can kiss me and dad goodnight."

"Wow...you have that down. Remind me not to get on the wrong side of you?"

"Oh, Russ, I'm not mad, that is just how I do it. I've tried acting sweet; it doesn't work. For now this is the best I can do."

For about five minutes the house was completely quiet. Then it started just a little murmur, but the noise level was tolerable.

There was a little disturbance near the bathroom. "**Mom! Mom**, Anthony has been in the bathroom forever."

With her hands on her hips, standing in the middle of the living room, "Anthony are you sick? Do you need some medicine?"

A voice muffled by the bathroom door and running water, "No, I'll be out as soon as I dry off."

Denny's reply, "Yeah but he is using all the hot water."

Jacquelyn coming around the corner from the bedrooms with her hands up walked hesitantly to her father. Looking up at him and raising her hands, "Daddy?"

"Yes Jackie, I'm your daddy." Reaching down and placing her on his lap, "Are we friends now?"

Naomi sticking her head in one of the bedrooms, "Denny, Anthony are you ready for bed?"

In unison, "Yes mam."

"Well come out here and say goodnight to your dad."

With Jackie in his lap Russell looked up to see the boys. "Mom and I will tuck you guys in. Call after you say your prayers, do you need me in there to make sure you pray? Remember to thank God for bringing me home safe."

Denny with his lips in a pout and Anthony with his hands hanging loosely in front of him "Yes mam."

Turning to Russell, "I've got a little toddler's bed set up for Jackie in the room next to ours. Don't freak, but sometimes she'll climb into bed with me."

The night he had been thinking about, planning for over a year was not at all what he had expected, and he was evidently not the only one disappointed.

Turning their backs to one another, but for Russell sleep would not come. Putting his head close to Naomi's and listening. He could hear her steady deep breathing.

Pulling the sheets back and getting up Russ tried to ease out of bed. As quietly as he could he crept into the kitchen. With the refrigerator door open he was startled when he felt Naomi standing behind him, "I'm sorry. There's cold water in the fridge?"

"It feels as if I've got a mouthful of cotton. I guess that's better than sand? Listen I am sorry."

Standing next to Russ, Naomi forced a smile. Rusty, it has been a long time. It's OK. Russ looking in the fridge, "I see we still have some iced tea. Is it sweet tea?"

"Yeah I still can't use to unsweetened tea. Since when did you quit smoking?"

"Evidently too soon. Although this is a first for me, but I could use a cigarette right now."

Putting ice in two glasses, and pouring tea, almost dropping the glasses, "I don't know what's wrong with me. One night about two months ago I ran out of smokes. I decided not to buy anymore. They just didn't taste right, so I quit."

"You said we were going to visit your folks, but you never said when?"

"I guess we need to make that trip to Houston soon. I was thinking we could leave after the weekend. Of course I can go alone."

"No way mister. Plus your folks haven't seen the baby yet. You know your dad has cancer. We may never get another chance for the kids to be with him."

"Well he didn't act like he needed to see us right away. Plus we probably should wait until we find out when he's going into surgery."

"The boys will be on Easter vacation in a week. Maybe we could plan the trip for during Easter vacation."

"I'll call mom tomorrow and tell her our plans."

Grabbing Russell's hand, "Let's go back to bed. Don't worry just hold me? You know I did miss you."

The first rays of light were coming through the window. Russ pulled Naomi close him, "Now I think I could use that cigarette."

Pushing her hair out of her eyes, "What time is it?" Squinting at the clock radio on the dresser, "Oh! Shit we got to get the boys ready for school."

Jackie was the first to show up in the kitchen. "Mommy, Yum, Yum.

Pointing to the cupboard, "There's cerul up there, daddy." Jackie said.

Turning to Russell, Naomi added, "The bowls are in the cupboard next to the pantry."

Denny came out of the bedroom, needing his hair combed, and his shoelaces tied. Anthony sat at the table in front of his cereal. Russell noticed something wrong with his shirt. He had a clip on tie, and a shirt with a collar, but he had only buttoned the top two buttons. Jackie still had her pink pajamas with pictures of blue bunnies. Without even turning Naomi picked her up and placed her in the highchair.

Heading for the bathroom Naomi turned back, and stopped, "Russ, do you think you could find your old elementary school?"

"Denny, Anthony, are you boys ready?"

Blue collared shirt, with clip on tie, and shirt tail hanging outside his gray slacks Anthony headed for the car with Russ trailing. With eyebrows raised, "OK Anthony, where is your brother?"

"He had to go to the bafroom."

Opening the car doors directing Anthony in the back seat, climbing behind the steering wheel, and turning, "Buckle up now." Leaning over the front seat tapping his father on the shoulder, "Daddy, Daddy. I dreameded about you when you were away."

"I thought I told you to buckle up?"

"I will daddy, when Denny gets here. Did you hear me daddy. I dreamded about you when you were in the war."

Looking back at his son, "Well you know I dreamed about you too."

"Was you scared when the road exploded in front of you and blew up? What was that smell? My eyes burned it was so bright, and my nose was burning. It was burning so bad that my eyes hurt and I was crying. You were really brave dad."

"Anthony, did your mom tell you about that explosion?"

Thinking about the night he ran to the bunker, *"I don't remember writing about that night. I know because I didn't want to worry Naomi. There are weird things going on with my body I haven't been sleeping well, and I **am** forgetting things. Maybe I did write about it?"*

"Did your mom tell you about that?" just as Denny showed up.

"Sorry dad, but I didn't think I could hold it."

"School still start at eight?"

"Yes sir, but we meet in church and then walk to school with the class." Denny replied. "Well, we still have time."

Russell stopped at the curb in front of the church watching his boys run up the steps to the double doors of the church, and somewhere in the back of his mind he was remembering lugging his newly covered text books up those steps. He could see in his mind's eye getting up early to serve mass. Things have certainly changed. Looking back at the two story red brick building that was his school. He didn't ask his wife if they still separated the boys and the girls; with the boys on one side of the building and the girls on the other.

There was a small woman walking up the sidewalk towards the church. She had a pale blue skirt, white blouse and what looked like a blue scarf. She turned to look at him and he could see the large rosaries at her waist and the cross around her neck.

Still what Anthony told him this morning was gnawing at is mind. *"I still have all the letters Naomi sent me. They are in a cigar box I kept in my duffel bag. Now in the bottom of my dresser drawer. I need to look through them to see if she mentions that night so long ago in another world. Yet it was only twelve months ago."*

Calling the boys back to the car. Denny looking out of breath, "What's the matter dad." Pointing to the woman in the pale blue dress. "Is that one of your teachers?"

Both boys turned to look. Anthony answered, "No, I think she is a nun. My teacher is not a nun."

Denny chimed in, "Mine neither."

Chapter 2

Putting his large callused hands up to his eyes, squinting against the glare from the sun through a dirt crusted windshield, Melvin Wright watched as he opened the door of the van as beer cans tumble out. Turning his large frame from behind the steering wheel, and swinging his booted feet and long legs out of the door. Putting his arms around his bare chest with a shiver against the cold he unzipped the fly of his stained khaki pants and urinated. Pulling his fly up and reaching back in the van feeling around for the dash, and finally grabbing a crumpled cigarette pack, and finding one bent cigarette. He found his cigarette lighter stuck in the crease of the front seat cushion. Unsuccessfully trying to light the cigarette. After several tries finally putting the tip of his finger over the hole in the cigarette. Drawing in the sweet smoke. With a coughing spasm, sticking his head back in the van and looking back. Taking a breath after the coughing stopped. He saw Darlene lying in the empty cargo area in a fetal position with both hands holding her stomach. She was moaning. Her moans were soft, he could barely hear them. If it weren't for the convulsive like shaking he would not have known she had been moaning. Beside Darlene was an empty syringe, she still had a rubber like tube around her arm just above her elbow.

Banging on the side of the cargo van, Melvin yelled, "Darlene! Darlene get up we have to move." Moving away from the van he felt his well-worn boots sink in the mud. He also felt the mud seeping up around his toes. Shouting to the back of the van, "Darlene, Did Larry call?"

Coughing up phlegm and spiting before she spoke, "Melvin, where are we?"

"I'm not sure. There are a lots of trees, shrubs, and it looks like a Cypress next to a river. It sure don't smell like roses here, more like a backed up sewer. I asked if you got any calls on that cell phone."

"It's not working."

"What do you mean it's not working?"

"Oh a message pops up saying I need to make a payment."

"Ah shit."

Cupping his hands and holding them above his eyes, "I think I see a shack on stilts. Looks like the shack is sitting right over the water."

Just then there was a screech, and the flutter of wings. Darlene screamed, "What was that?"

Looking up, Melvin saw a large white bird, with black tipped wings. Reaching into the van, and grabbing the tee shirt that was roll up in a ball under the front seat, sniffing the shirt and pulling it over his head, "I think that was a crane." Still watching the crane as it climbed into the air he saw several white ibis stalking through the grass near the shore line of the river in their jerky-leggy way, looking Melvin assumed for bugs and worms Grabbing a roll of toilet paper, pushing the doors at the rear of the van open, forcing unkempt mousy brown hair away from her eyes, and running for one of the higher growing shrubs, she looked over at Melvin with a look of pain. "Melvin, I don't feel so good. You think you might be able to get me some paregoric

"Darlene, I don't know where we are. I remember passing the sign for Slidell, and then Tammany Parish."

Coughing and clearing more phlegm from her throat, "You think maybe you could get me some *Scat*?"

"Baby, like I said, I don't know where **here** is, and even if I did we don't have any money."

Coming out from behind the shrub, pulling her jeans up, and making an effort to straighten her blue tank top, "Baby you always know how to take care of me. You have any beer left. It might just settle my stomach."

Climbing behind the wheel and motioning for Darlene to get in the van, "We need to get out of this damn swamp."

Three tries and the engine finally turned over. Stepping on the gas did nothing, but make the back wheels spin, digging the van deeper in the mud. "Foregut me." Looking over at Darlene, "Get over here behind the wheel. I'll push. Just wait until I tell you, and then step on the gas, not hard but easy."

The wheels still spinning, "Darlene, put it in reverse, then in drive." Now the wheels were digging in in both directions.

Sticking her head out of the window, "Now, what?"

"Grab our packs. Let's go over to that shack. I don't think there's anyone there." A gurgle as Darlene tried to clear her throat, "Then what are we going to do?"

"Maybe we can find a shovel, or some rocks or maybe a two-by-four. Something to use to get us out of the mud." Melvin did find an Army issue pick and shovel in the shack.

The sun was high in the sky by the time they got the van free of the mud. Back in the shack, over the water. He remembered seeing several cans on a shelf, mostly beans. Digging his Swiss Army knife out of his packet and using the can opener attachment he opened a can of beans, he and Darlene took turns putting the can to their lips sucking the beans out of the can.

Digging into Darlene's large hand bag, Melvin managed to find a hair brush and managed to get his black, gray specked hair back and with the use of a scrunchy he found in Darlene's hand bag he put his hair in his usual ponytail.

Looking out the doorway, and back at Melvin, "It's hot. Do you think that river water is cold? Ya know, maybe we could clean up a little? I feel a little better."

With a lot of awes and OH's they managed to splash enough river water on their naked bodies and face to get most of the grime off, and by splashing under their arms to lessen some of smell.

Sitting down in the river water, letting the water come up to his chin. "Come over here Darlene this was your idea." It was then that Melvin stood up, "Hey baby did you hear that?"

"Hear what?"

"I thought I heard a splash."

"That was you."

"Oh! Funk! Move get out of the water."

"What is it?"

Pointing to the shore line. "Look over there. About fifty feet down there on the shore line."

Cuffing her hand above her eyes. "All I see is an old log down there."

"Darlene that ain't no log. That is a gator, and I think we woke him up from his nap." Grabbing Darlene by the back of her neck. "Move Darlene. I think he's pissed."

Without actually running they both made it to the shack and what looked to Melvin like a gator that had to be a least twenty feet long.

Taking a deep breath, digging jeans out of his back pack, "Put some clothes on Darlene. Let us try and find a town

Backing up on the muddy track, carefully turning the van and slowly moving under Spanish moss laden oak trees. The van started sliding momentarily, the wheels finally grabbing traction as they entered a two lane asphalt road.

Reaching for the crumbled cigarette pack, feeling inside the crumbled pack, and letting out a sigh of frustration. Glancing at Darlene, "I think I remember seeing a sign for Pearl River. I don't know whether it was just the name of a river, or a town, but if there are enough people I'm sure we can score something."

"Like some *Scat*?"

With sarcasm, "Darlene would you please knock it off about your medicine."

"I'm sorry Melvin. I am feeling a little better."

Sticking his hands first in his front pockets, then in his rear pockets, in his thread bare shirt pocket, and finally tearing through his canvass wallet he found a small piece of paper. I need to call Larry. He said he'd call me. But our phone don't work! He has probably been trying to reach us."

"How you gona get hold of this guy. I mean you never been here before. Have you?"

"No I don't think so, but I do have this guy Larry's," pointing to the small piece of paper, "phone number. Good thing I saved his number. I didn't worry cause he was supposed to call us."

"Melvin, when I miss my medicine I get a bad stomach ache. Sometimes I have diarrhea so bad that I don't think I'll ever get off the toilet."

Putting his hand up as if to stop her from talking, "I know baby, I'll get something for you. Now just shut up about your belly ache."

"Melvin, this time is worse than ever. It even hurts when I try to pee. It looks like I'm peeing coke cola."

"OK. You want me to find you a doctor. You know we can check into the Emergency Room. They got to take you."

"I'll be quiet." With a groan, and a sigh, "If we go to the hospital they will put me in re-hab, or worse."

"Hey, re-hab's not that bad. The food is not all that good, but they do feed you."

Deep ditches on both sides of the black asphalt highway. Shrub growing on the sides of the deep ditches. Oak trees with Spanish moss hanging down almost to the road; looking like an archway. Looking down at the speedometer Melvin notices the engine light flashing low fuel, suddenly what sounds like a fart. He looks over at Darlene. She raises her shoulders mouthing the words. All of a sudden they both hear a clunk, followed by a clank. The van shivered. The sound of corn popping. The van threatens to die. Then it does die. He tried to restart the engine only to hear several clicks. Melvin manages to coast over as far as he can without sliding into the ditch.

In the haze of the sun, humidity and heat Melvin makes out what looks like old fashioned gas pumps. Motioning for Darlene to slide out of the van through the driver's side, "Darlene I see a gas station up the road. Let's get us some gas, and maybe just a little cash."

Following Melvin out of the van, "Melvin, how we gona do that."

Walking closer to the gas pumps, looking first to the right and then to the left. There's a sign above what looks like a little convenience store. "Darlene see that sign. I can't read it can you?"

"Yeah Melvin."

"Well baby what does it say?"

With a little giggle, "It says sandwiches, beer and bait."

"Well Darlene, I sure would like a nice cold beer."

"But Melvin. We ain't got no money."

Opening his eyes wide, putting his hands on his cheeks, with irony "Darlene you know what to do. You just bat your eyes and I'll borrow us a little cash, and maybe get some gas for the van."

The little bait shack and gas station looked to be about maybe a quarter mile, but wiping sweat off is brow Melvin thought it might as well be a hundred miles. The gravel on the side of the road was working its way into the holes in the bottom of his boots. Darlene was walking slower and slower, until Melvin finally stopped and looked back at her. "Darlene, you want to get somthen for that pain in your belly"?

Taking a deep breath bending over and putting her hands on her knees, "Yes Melvin. Don't be mad. Just give me a sec to catch my breath."

"OK Darlene." Pointing to a large Spanish moss covered oak tree closest to the road, and a few feet away from the drainage ditch, "See that oak tree?"

Darlene looking down the road, squinting against the glare of the sun, "Melvin…" clearing her throat, "There are a lot of trees."

"Well Darlene," with sarcasm, "it's the big one on this side of the ditch." Walking over to the tree and sitting cross legged Melvin proceeded to pull off his left boot, rubbing his toes, and shaking a pebble out of the boot. He pulled his gray sock up and put the boot back on.

"Five minutes. We got to get out of the sun."

Squatting against the tree, sniffling, looking up at Melvin, "Thank you Melvin. Just give me a few minutes."

"Melvin, don't you find it weird that we haven't seen any traffic on this road. Where are we anyway? I don't see no signs."

"Kinda, no I haven't, and I have no idea."

"What?" trying to get to her feet, and looking around.

"No Darlene I ain't seen no traffic, and I haven't even seen a mile marker. Yes it is kind a weird. I wonder if there's gona be anyone in that bait shop, but if you look down towards the river there a few small cabins; must be that fishing camp we saw on the sign a ways back."

Almost out of breath Darlene walked up to the door with what may have been at one time painted white, but appeared to be chipped dull yellow. Breathing heavily, "What now Melvin?"

Let out a long sigh, "You go in first. I'll just go around back. I need to take a leak."

"What am I supposed to do?"

"You know what to do. Looks like there's only one person in there. Give him a sad story. You know how your car broke down and how you think you got the flu or somthen. Tell him you need gas for the car."

Behind a counter with a cash register in the middle, fishing lures on a peg board behind the counter. At the end of the counter near a wall next to a tank with live bait was fishing rods and poles with nets on the end. There was a tall skinny boy with his back turned to Darlene. With her hands on the counter "Excuse me sir. Excuse me."

Darlene looked up at the man, and found herself looking at the biggest Adam's apple she had ever seen; it was almost obscene, or a very large tumor.

Looking down directly into her eyes, "Cher how can I help you?"

No matter how pitiful she tried to sound, the tall skinny man with the biggest Adam's apple she ever saw, and hair like yellow straw sticking out of a John Deer ball cap, would not give an inch. "Cher, I can let ya use the phone, but I be the ony one here. Can't leave. You want to buy something? "

As the skinny man turned back to the shelf, Melvin casually walked in. he slid behind the counter and with his Swiss Army knife, the large blade out he grabbed the man's head pushed it forward and down and drew the blade just over his large Adam's apple.

Banging on the register the drawer finally opened. Melvin looked in the drawer, looked over at Darlene, "Awe funk, I don't even think there's fifty bucks here."

Darlene just stood staring at the boy... man sliding down to the floor. "Melvin did you have to do that?"

"What? I discovered that if you put the head down the neck won't spirt blood."

"No Melvin. Did you have to kill him?"

"Well he said nobody else was here. Grabbing a couple packs of cigarettes, handing the bills he just pulled out of the register to Darlene. I'll get us one of them gas cans. Maybe we can get enough gas to get down the road." Now there is no one to tell nobody what we look like."

Walking back towards their van, Darlene called, "Wait up. Why couldn't I wait at the store for you? You know I'm sick."

"You want to be there when somebody does show up? I should have grabbed a cold six pack. Trouble bein if someone did happen to drive by and saw be luggen a six pack, they just might get a little suspicious."

"Now you can go back to that bait shack if you want, but what if one of them fishermen decides he needs more bait. Well do you want to go back and wait?"

Whining like a child that has been punished, "Noo."

After several tries Melvin got the van started. "Well Darlene you gona stand out there or get in the van."

"I'm getting in."

Driving by the bait shack Melvin shook Darlene, "Look over there." There were two cars with flashing blue and red lights attached to a bar on the roof of their cars, and state decals on the doors. "I was kinda hopen we could fill up the tank, maybe get a six pack. A cold beer would be great."

Finally on an interstate highway. "Darlene! Darlene, wake up!"

"What is it Melvin?"

"How much money you got?"

"I got whatever you gave me."

Sighing, "Well Darlene how much did I give you?"

"Oh..." Digging into her hand bag, Let me count it." Holding the bills and counting one at a time. "It looks like about sixty-three dollars."

"About? Well is it sixty-three dollars or not?" Counting again, "Yeah, Melvin. It's sixty-three dollars."

Putting both hands of the wheel, and looking towards the right, and then leaning closer to the windshield, "I see a sign saying there was food and gas at the next exit. I hope that exit ain't too far."

"Melvin," With that irritating nasal sound, "Melvin, you past the exit."

"Awe, shit." Literally yanking the steering wheel to the right, wheels spinning in the loose sand and gravel on the side of the road.

Turning sharply, and turning in the opposite directions, as the blaring of horns reminding him that he was heading the wrong way. He did notice several people with their middle finger up. He didn't have to be a lip reader to understand some of what the people were saying.

Darlene holding on to the hand hold above the passenger side window, "Mellvin…I don't want to die."

With the van teetering in a precarious position, finally righting, "Stop your whining. We made it."

Walking into the gas station convenience store, looking at the counter and then around the store. There had to be at least a dozen people wandering the isles or waiting for a sandwich at the deli counter at the back of the store. He walked up to the clerk and handed him fifty dollars. Looking up at the freckled red headed clerk, "I'm at pump three. Not sure how much it will take."

After pumping forty dollars' worth in the tank, sticking his head in the window. "I didn't fill it but I think we got enough gas to get to the next town."

Pushing her hair back away from her eyes and licking her lips, "Do we have enough left over for my medicine?"

Glancing at Darlene, looking into eyes sunken so deeply that all he could see were two deep dark holes, her cough had become almost rhythmic she was holding a dirty rag up to her running nose, "Darlene, you couldn't even get a taste for ten dollars, but we just might be able to get a cold six pack. Once we get to town I'll be better able to figure out how we can get some money."

"Melvin, if you let me go inside, I'm sure I can find some man that will help us out."

"No Darlene. We don't need to draw attention to ourselves. Besides I don't like to see you doin that no more."

"You just don't think I look good enough anymore."

"Just hang in there. Once we get to some town I'll give Larry a call. Then he'll send us enough money to get what we need."

Chapter 3

Russell coming up behind Naomi as she is putting a wrapped sandwich and an apple in a baggy and then in a brown paper lunch bag, "Just where do you think you're going?"

Turning her head so that Russ can give her a peck on the cheek, "I thought I better get it over with. You know Jack has been pretty good with me. He's put up with me taking off when I had to take one of the kids to the doctor. I think I owe it to him to give a two week notice."

"Believe me I'd love to have you home," Pulling one chair out from under the kitchen table, motioning for Naomi to sit. Pulling another chair out and setting it next to her, "Naomi, we need to talk."

Sitting on the edge of the chair like she was about to run a race, "Russ we'll have plenty of time to talk, but I really don't want to be late. I'm going to be asking for a couple weeks off. Plus I'll put in my notice." Taking a deep breath then letting it out, "This will only take a minute. What I tried to tell you last night is that you can quit that's fine with me, but if you'd like to keep your job for a while that's fine too."

Sounding a little frustrated and pursing her lips, "Listen mister, when you joined the Air Force we agreed that we as a family would go wherever you went if we could. You know when the orders say accompanied I intend to be the one that does the accompanying."

"Well I thought maybe I could commute."

Looking up and raising her eyebrows, "OK. What's up?"

"I tried to tell you that my new assignment is right across the bay. I've already been communicating with my sponsor. Rumor has it that I'll probably be the new NCOIC of Base Operations.

Naomi jumped up and put her arms around his neck.

"Now lady if you really like that job of yours you better get. Don't forget to ask for two weeks around Easter."

"Since I didn't go in yesterday I'm not sure what time I'll get off. Would you drop me off at work, and take the kids to school. Oh yeah you'll need to pick them up. I'll call you when I ready for a ride. Oh if you want you don't to put Jackie in day-care. That's if you think you're up to taking care of a three year old."

With a start, Russ looked up, "Where did Anthony go?"

Pointing to the driveway, "that's him. Looks like he is putting the car seat in."

Russ gently moves Anthony out of the way. Exasperated after several tries at getting the car seat fastened in the back seat, Dennis finally comes and with little effort fastens the seat in the middle of the back seat. "OK wise guy, slide in the backseat. We'll drop you guys off first."

"I thought mom wanted to go in to work first?"

Looking over at Naomi, then the boys, "Naomi, what time do you need to be at work?"

"Jack likes his office staff in by nine. The partners stagger in whenever."

"Are you one of the partners?"

Raising her eyes, "No Russell, I am not a partner. I deal with some people mainly people that are filing Bankruptcy The rest of the time I file records and do some typing."

"OK. We take the kids in first. After all you work downtown, and if I'm not mistaken their school is less than ten minutes from here."

Tapping Anthony on the shoulder what are your waiting for?" Pointing to the back seat. "OK you guys climb in the back with your sister."

Naomi placing her hand on Russ' knee, "What would you say to Tuna Casserole for supper? If you haven't change too much I seem to remember that you preferred not eating meat on Fridays."

"Sounds great. You doin a casserole or salad?"

"I was thinking of the casserole."

"The Tuna Helper out of the box?"

"No. Tuna helper wouldn't even satisfy Jackie. Your kids are no pikers when it comes to eating. I had a girlfriend over for dinner, and when she saw how much they ate, she said she would rather clothe them then feed them any day."

At the table and watching his kids eat, Russ jumped up after the last plate was empty and the casserole dish was empty and cleared the table.

"Russell I would have cleaned the table. Just relax. Your time will come."

"I was afraid they would eat the plates. Did you see how fast I moved my hands?" Denny, sitting at the table with his hands neatly folded and looking up at his dad. "Can we get up now?

Looking at the kids, Naomi said with just a little wonder in her voice, "Since when do you wait for permission to leave the table. I'm not complaining. As a matter of fact I would like to see that all the time"

With his elbows on the table and leaning on his hands, Anthony remarked, "Just waiting for dad to tell us when we're taking our trip."

Jackie still in her highchair, wiping her face with the back of her hand, and looking first at her brothers then at her dad.

"Well Anthony you're right, but you know we are taking a trip to visit your grandparents. I just wanted to tell you that we will be here for Sunday mass, but early Monday we are taking off for Houston."

With a burp, Anthony looked at his mom and then his dad, "We really won't be leaving till Tuesday."

Turning to face her second son and wiping her hands on a dish towel, "Anthony! Why would you say that?"

"Cause daddy will need to get some medicine on Monday."

"Why would you say that?" Russell replied.

"Cause you will, but we'll still get to go on Tuesday."

Taking charge Naomi once again sounding like a drill sergeant, "OK boys. You can watch television for a little while," reaching down for Jackie, "and you young lady need a bath."

With her hands up above her head, waiting to be picked up, "Me watch tee bee too." Pulling her little undershirt off, "Well young lady we'll see."

Plopping down in the big overstuffed recliner, and looking over at the boys, who if they were any closer would literally have their noses glued to the screen, "Slide back about five feet, and by the way

Anthony what did you mean we would have to wait for me to get my medicine?"

Denny broke in, "Well daddy if Anthony says we got to wait for you to get your medicine; we will have to wait until you get your medicine."

"The only medicine I have ever taken was an aspirin."

The boys fell asleep in front of the TV, Jackie was just about asleep when Naomi lifted her out of the tub.

Pulling the sheets back Russell looked over at Naomi, "I don't know why I'm so keyed up. I mean I spent over a year in the desert. If anything this trip should be like a walk in the park"

Climbing into the bed and scooting up against Russell, "Aw... Your feet are cold. It really isn't cold at all. It has been up in the 80s all day, it ain't that much lower now."

"Sorry, but that's been happening a lot lately. When I get a few minutes I going to have to see a doctor bout that. I never had a problem with circulation before."

"You know Russ that's the reason I married you." Russell turning towards her with raised eyebrows. "You know I was looking for a warm body to snuggle up against."

"I do hope you found other attributes other than a warm body."

"Oh yeah. Which reminds me. Did you and your dad have a good relationship?"

"Not really. Oh my dad wasn't abusive, or anything. I just don't think he liked me very much."

"Didn't you guys ever do things together? You know, like play catch, or go fishing together. Did he ever take you to a ball game; like you do with the boys? Remember you took Denny and Anthony to watch the Yankees."

"I think we may have gone to a ballgame. But if we did it was rare."

"Me and my dad were never close. I tried. I was ten when he retired from the Army. You know what I think is worse than abuse? I think being ignored is worse. I always got the impression that he didn't like me. The only reason I agreed to this trip is because of mom."

Throwing the sheets back Russ pushes himself up, feeling some stiffness in his left shoulder. Thinking he probably slept on it wrong. He swung around with more than a little more effort than he expected. Finally sitting on the side of the bed. Pain shot up his legs as he tried to stand. He couldn't close his hands, which looked like balloons. He tried again to stand, but fell back down on the side of the bed. Calling out, "Naomi! Naomi, where are you?"

A muffled sound from behind the closed bathroom door, "Russ I'll be right out just give me a minute." The sound of the toilet flushing, then a squeak as the bathroom door opened. Without looking up, "Russ remind me to call someone when we get back to fix that dor…" looking at her husband sitting on the edge of the bed, "What in the world happened to you?"

"I don't know, but I can't stand, or close my hands."

Bending down, and attempting to help Russ to his feet, "Can you try to stand?"

"Naomi there is no way you are going to be able to lift me."

"The number for the Base clinic is by the phone in the living room." While waiting Russell did manage to clumsily limp into the bathroom.

With just a little panic in her voice, Russ, I called the Air Force Hospital. They told me to take you to the E.R. here in St. Pete. They said if you can't walk I was to call an Ambulance."

"I think I can make it to the car. What about the kids?"

"The car seat is still in the car."

Walking into the boys room Naomi's eyes opened wide as she looked the boys were dressed, and Denny had his sister in his room trying to help her get dressed. "What's going on boys?"

"Anthony woke me up, and told me we was goin to the hospital with you and dad."

"Thank you so much for getting the baby ready. We have to take dad to the emergency room. Evidently they don't believe in emergencies over at the air base." With a sigh Naomi walked back into her bedroom noticing that Russ was not there. "Russ are you here?"

"Yeah, Naomi. I'm in the bathroom. Be out in a sec."

Walking over to the bathroom door, sticking her head in the door then holding her nose. "Woo! That ain't roses. Are you able to walk now?"

""Yeah. It's weird. My ankle hurts, but not really that bad. It's like my feet are numb, but the pain is almost tolerable; it's just that I don't have control I'm unsteady." Looking pulling his trousers up, and attempting to pull his fly up; without much luck. "Look at my hands. You ever take one of those rubber gloves and blow it up like a balloon? Well?" Holding his hand up in front of Naomi, "I wonder if I could make a balloon animal out of my hands."

"You are not funny mister. Now come over here; if you can, and let me pull the zipper of your fly up."

After a shot of some sort of steroid, and sent home a Zithromax Z-PAK, Russ was told to go home and rest. As for a diagnoses, the medicos could not come up with anything other than influenza of the joints and for him to promise he would contact his personal physician.

Within a half hour the swelling in his hands had gone down and he was able to close his fist. Everyone was thrilled when Russ talked Naomi to stopping in at the local I-Hop. Eggs sausage, hash browns, and pancakes for the boys, little pancakes in the shape of Mickey Mouse for Jacquelyn, eggs Benedict for Naomi, and chicken fingers and waffles for Russ.

A walk around Mirror Lake, Jackie chasing the ducks, and back to the house. Russ reassured everyone that he was feeling fine and they would start their trip to Houston in the morning.

By 5:30 in the PM Jackie was holding her tummy and crying. Russ called her over to him and told her to sit in his lap. "Naomi, we got any Sprite in the fridge?"

"Yeah."

"Pour a small glass let it sit for a few minutes. As soon as it gets to room temperature bring it to me."

With the glass in his hand Russ placed the glass near Jackie's lips, "Now Jackie Daddy wants you to drink this."

With her lips tight and a little cajoling she finally opened her mouth, and held the glass, first sipped than drank the little bit of Sprite in one gulp. Within seconds Jackie lets out a burp and a little fart. "Daddy I feel better now."

That night the kids appeared to be bouncing off the walls. Russ could swear he could see the energy in the room. By nine the silence was overwhelming. Watching some sitcom; wasn't really paying attention he turned to his wife, "Now I'm keyed up."

Naomi getting up and heading for the bedroom, "Russell, I think I can help you. Come on get yourself a nice hot shower, and come to bed."

Chapter 4

Pulling next to one of two gas pumps in front of a convenience store, Melvin turned to Darlene, "Well baby you know what to do."

Feeling phlegm in the back of her throat, Darlene manage to hack it up and spit out the window. Wiping her mouth, "Melvin I don't like doing that. I'm cramping real bad. Do you think they'll let me use the toilet in there?"

"Darlene, that is gross."

"I know that's why I don't like doing that."

"Not that, but spitting out the window is gross. I think it's some kinda health law where they have a public restroom; especially where they sell food"

Wiping her mouth, and opening the door, "Oh."

"While you're at it wipe off the side of the door too."

As she opened the door to the little convenience store, the bell hooked to the top of the door rang. Darlene looked up with a start. As she looked over at the counter her heart felt as if it stopped when she saw two policemen leaning against the counter sipping a steaming beverage out of a paper cup. The clerk looked up and the policemen, the blond one with a buzz cut, the other very tall with dark hair, turned to stare at her. With a hard swallow, "Excuse me. I think we're lost."

Just as the police officer started to answer, Melvin walked in, "Sorry did I interrupt something?

Digging into a large ice chest Melvin pulled out a beer. "That road gets my throat mighty parched."

The taller of the two policemen spoke up, "You're not thinken of drinking that while you're driving are you?"

"

"No sir. We were planning of camping when we got through town."

"Well this ain't much of a town." Looking over at the clerk, "There's a nice little campsite about eleven miles out of town. That is if you are heading north. Don't get many people camping this time of year. Now next month the campers will be coming in force."

"Well, thanks. Me and the misses will be headen for the camp grounds." Looking over at the clerk, a small framed teenager with acne scars on his face, "You wouldn't happen to have a phone I could use?"

The smaller blond police officer turned and with raised eyebrows, "Sorry I'm Deputy Wilson." Pointing to the taller one, "This here is Deputy Samson. Most folks today carry cell phones. I'm sure Daryl can let you use the phone if it's a locale call."

"Got one, but the carrier would like payment before they turn it on. No sir it's not local. It's to my employer, but it is a 1-800 number."

Pointing to the back of the store behind the display counters, "Ya know I got cell phones here that only cost ten bucks."

Darlene just staring at Melvin. Melvin looking at the deputies and then at Daryl, "Not this time but maybe later. That's kinda why I need to call my boss. We had a little car trouble and I need to get an advance on my pay."

As Melvin headed back towards the payphone the tall deputy spoke up, "If I ever called the lieutenant to tell him I needed an advance, after he finished laughing he'd tell me to walk."

Motioning for Darlene to come closer the tall cop asked, "You feeling alright lady?" Trying to keep from looking in the deputy's eyes, "Yeah, well no. I think I might have the stomach flu. Maybe I just ate something that isn't agreeing with me."

The clerk pointed to the back of the store, "There's a public restroom back there." Walking back toward the restrooms, Darlene called back to Melvin, "Mel, I'll wait out in the van."

Holding his hand over the mouthpiece of the telephone, "OK, Darlene."

"Darlene, is that your name, Darlene?" Daryl asked. "Yeah, I mean yes."

Coming out of the restroom and looking up, not seeing Melvin.

The clerk pointed to the door, "The Coffee's free. Take a cup with you." Once back in the van, and within minutes Darlene was asleep.

Melvin had to shake Darlene to wake her, "I got hold of Larry. He said that we can pick up two grand at eight tomorrow morning. Said that he'll wire it to us. Will be able to pick the money up at any Super Walmart."

Sitting up and leaning forward Darlene started hacking until she was able to clear the phlegm from her throat. She opened the door and spit." Taking a stained handkerchief from her purse she wiped her lips, and turned to Melvin, "I didn't get any of that nastiness on your van."

"You still feeling bad. I notice you are sweating. It really ain't that hot. Matter a fact it's getting down right cold out here."

Starting to shake, unable to keep her hands steady, "Melvin you got any money left. Maybe enough to get me a little taste."

"Whatever money we got is in your purse, but I don't think you'll find any."

"Where did you get the money to pay for the beer?"

"I kept five out just for something like that."

"You can afford a beer, but I can't get what I need?"

"It's a good thing I did. It would have sure made those cops suspicious if I came in there without getting somthen."

"Which way is north?" banging his hands on the steering wheel, "And where the hell is a Walmart?"

Pulling into a gas station that was lit up like an airport runway, "Darlene go in there and find out where the closest Walmart is."

Sweat covering her brow, Darlene opens the passenger side door, climbing up into the seat, "The lady behind the counter said the closet Walmart is back towards Slidell."

"Did you ask about a Western Union?"

"No. You didn't tell me to."

After making several stops for Darlene. They tried to stop at the roadside rest areas, and then pulling off on to the shoulder and shielding Darlene with the van door. A trip that should have taken less than an hour, took them almost two hours. They were finally at a 24 hour Walmart.

"Why are you parking so far from the doors?"

"Well if I know Walmart there a probably cameras in their parking lot. I don't really think we can pick up our money until morning"

After several trips to the restroom inside the Walmart, the sun shining through the van window, Darlene shook Melvin, "Is it time yet to pick up our money."

Stretching and popping the door open, looking at his watch, "It's not quite time, but maybe somebody will be there to check on the MoneyGram?"

Coming out of the restroom Darlene notices that Melvin is sleeping on the bench right inside the entrance. Darlene shakes him. "Melvin I think the bank is open."

A skinny blond middle aged woman with her back turned to the counter, putting paper bands around stacks of money, turned to face Melvin. With a look as if she smelled something bad, asked, "How may I help you this morning?"

Walking up to the counter, the blond woman stepping back like she might catch something, Melvin replied, "Sorry. Do you handle Western Union?"

"No we don't but Customer Service is right next door, they can send a telegram for you.

There were quite a few people in line at Customer Service. When Melvin finally got up to the counter, "Mam, do you handle Western Union?"

With a sigh and moving little closer to the counter, "Yes. Do you need to send a telegram?"

"No. My boss is supposed to wire me some money."

"Wester Union is not really open yet, but I can check and see if there is a wire for you. Do you have a picture I.D.?"

"Yeah, the license is from Montana, but I have my Social Security card also."

"I'm not sure if I can accept that. I'll need to talk to the manager."

Melvin could feel his face getting hot and the collar of his shirt starting to feel tight around his neck. Starting to hyperventilate, he deliberately forced himself to slow his breathing. "That's fine. I can wait. Where is your manager?"

"He should be coming through those doors any minute. Actually I thought he would already be here."

In the meantime Darlene was browsing around the pharmacy area, and she was surprised to see quaifensin DM, and Mucinex DM on the shelves. The last time she looked in other pharmacies they were keeping them behind the counter.

It was early and there were no pharmacist or anybody else working in that area. It was almost too easy. She had her large hand bag hanging off her shoulder. Looking right and left once more she approached the shelves with the Mucinex and quaifensin. While sliding the bottles of pills in her hand bag she noticed robitussin at the other end of the shelf. She threw several bottles into her bag.

A short fat balding man walked into the banking area and went behind the counter. The blond woman casually walks over to him, periodically looking up at Melvin than back at the bald man.

Walking, walking slowly back to the counter, she motions for Melvin to come to the counter. "My manager says that your license and Social Security card should be fine."

Darlene bending over the shelf with the Robitussin, scoops the entire shelf into her large hand bag. She then sees and scoots most of the shelf full of Vicks Nyquil in to her hand bag. She casually looks up and sees no one.

Glancing over at Melvin as he is counting money she casually walks out of the store. She senses more than sees someone behind her. Instinctively she heads away from the van.

Melvin walking out of Walmart notices an Asian man, built short and wide; reminding Melvin of a Samoan. The Samoan comes up on Darlene. He grabs her with thick stubby fingered hands by the shoulder. Melvin doesn't hear what he's saying, but he sees him reaching for handcuffs. Melvin moves quickly and silently. Pulls the Swiss Army knife out of his pocket, moves directly behind the Samoan, and with a thrust draws the knife across his neck. The knife barely penetrates the Samoan's thick neck. As the short thick man turns Melvin plunges the knife forward and forces the knife between his neck and his upper chest. Dark red almost black blood gurgles from his lips as the Samoan falls to the ground but for an instant he manages to rise, and grab for the knife. Melvin brings his right hand up and knocks the Samoan's hand away from his knife and pulls the knife out of the man's chest and then, as the Samoan is starting to get up again Melvin moves quickly and jabs the knife once again into the Samoan's torn bloody, throat. The Samoan's hands comes up to his throat. He covers his throat, Melvin can see coming out of his lips the blood coming between his fingers, and with a gurgle and blood Samoan falls to the asphalt parking lot. Putting his hands up to his throat as the blood seeps through his thick fingers.

Looking carefully right then left, not seeing anyone in the parking lot he tries to drag the man to the edge of the parking lot near some low bushes. Two tries at dragging the Asian with barely being able to move the body. Darlene turns and tries to help, they give up and leave him lying in the deserted part of the parking lot.

"OK, Darlene. What was that all about?"

Breathing heavily in between breaths, "I think he may have been upset with me for taking the cough medicine."

"OK, baby girl we need to get, and fast. You don't think they knew we were together?"

"That's why I walked right past you. So they wouldn't know we was together." Heading north on Route 11. Darlene speaks up. "Melvin do you know where we're goin? I think your speeding."

"No Darlene I ain't speeding. But we do need to head north, and I do believe we are heading north."

"Ya think we could stop so I could get my scat?"

"Let us get away from Slidell. There should be camp ground not far."

"Melvin, we still got that camping stove?"

The sun was getting brighter, Melvin could see steam coming of the road. "Yeah the stove is back there with our sleeping bags."

Traffic appeared to be light as they drove. It was a relief for Melvin to have quiet. Darlene reached over to turn on the radio. There wasn't much of a selection on the FM stations, there was nothing but static on the stations. Back on the AM dial. She heard the sounds of an accordion and a fiddle, the announcer saying something about the best Cajun and Zydeco music in Southwestern Louisiana. Melvin just looked at her and then at the radio. "Melvin, I still don't feel real good. I just needed somthen to distract me."

Looking back down at the radio and then at Darlene, "That's alright. What did you get at the Walmart?"

"Got me some pills. Would you believe that they had these pills on the shelves?" Letting out a long sigh, "What's so different about these pills?"

They stopped putting these pills on the shelves a while ago. Now they have to keep them back in the pharmacy. As soon as you can find a place off the highway I'll fix me some medicine."

"You can do that with those pills?"

"Yeah, but I need you to stop for a while so I can smash these pills. Then get some water and mix them real good."

Evening rush was just starting. The roads were not as crowded as expected. Leaning forward and squinting through the windscreen. He could see that it was getting dark and there were big black thunder clouds. Darlene had had her head back against the seat, her mouth was open and there was drool running down her chin when she woke with a start. Wiping her chin with the back of her hand, "Melvin, you're driving all over the road."

"I know the winds are picking up. You know this is what they call a high profile vehicle. When need to get off the road."

Turning the radio back on the announcer was saying how they were to expect a storm, and tornados have been spotted in the area of Pearl River. "You know Melvin that's probably why there isn't that many people on the road. Seems like a weather warning has been put out."

Creeping over to the right side of the road, "Darlene there was a sign back there that said there is a rest area not far up the road." Just then Melvin pulled over on the shoulder of the road and made an abrupt stop. Sticking is head out of the window and looking back down the road he put the van in reverse and drove about a half mile to the exit stating that the next rest stop is twenty miles.

Backing down the shoulder of the highway. It started to sprinkle, within seconds the sprinkle turned to large raindrops. The wind was gusting forcefully, it felt like they were at sea, as Melvin was trying in vain to keep the van on the shoulder of the road. The rains were now coming down in force. Melvin could barely see the entrance to the rest area. As he was pulling close to the public restrooms he looked over towards Darlene, who hadn't uttered a word since he started backing down the highway. Her eyes were closed tight, her lips were pressed together and rolled in so tightly that he barely saw them. Her cheeks were sucked in as if she were biting the inside. She was holding onto the handhold on above the door so tightly that her knuckles where beyond white, almost purple. "Darlene! It's alright. Relax, I'm going to stop here until the storm stops."

Backing into a parking spot in front of a low rock wall in front of the public restrooms. Darlene turned quickly to see red and blue lights flashing. "Melvin, I think there's a cop coming right behind us."

Melvin points to the rear of the van, "Darlene get in the back and stay quiet." Just as Darlene was pulling a blanket up around her shoulders and lying down near the rear cargo doors, there's a knock with the back of a large flashlight on the driver side window. Melvin cracks the window to notice a man the size of a bear, a very large bear, with a wide brim, Smokey Bear type hat with rain water pouring off the brim, and wearing a bright yellow raincoat. "Yes sir. What can I do for you?"

The trooper spoke with a deep thunderous voice, "Sir could I see your license and registration?"

"Is there a problem Trooper?"

"I don't think so. I just happen to see you backing up on the interstate."

Squinting through the rain into the partially opened window, "Just what are you, boy?"

"What do you mean?"

"Are you Mexican? Maybe Puerto Rican?"

"No sir. I'm Crow."

"Scooting up on the seat, and reaching into his back pocket for his wallet, attempting to pull his license out, the trooper held up his hand, "You don't have to pull it out just let me look at it."

"Wright don't sound like a Latino name."

"No sir, I'm Crow."

"Oh you mean you're some kind of Injun."

Taking a deep breath, and looking up at the trooper. "Sir, my registration is in the glove box."

"Is your proof of insurance in there too?"

"Yes sir."

Shining his flashlight through the window towards the back of the van, looking down at the license, "Mr. Wright, is someone in the back of the van?"

"Yes sir. That's Darlene. She isn't feeling well she's back there taking a nap."

"Can you call her up here?"

"Like I said she is not feeling well. I think it's some kinda woman problem. She might have trouble climbing over the seat."

"You want to walk back with me and open those doors?"

"Yes sir, but I'll need to pull up a little ways from that rock wall."

"OK Mr. Wright. Just keep your hands on the wheel until you move up a little." Backing away from the van the trooper started to walk to the back of the van.

With the rain dripping down from his Smoky Bear hat, and face, "Mr. Wright. Stick your right hand out you window and slowly open your door."

Rolling his window down leaning over to grab his keys, Melvin opened the door and eases himself out of the van. The rain pounding on his face, Melvin attempted to look at the trooper, "I can't see anything. I'm coming around the left side of the van. I've got the keys to the van in my hand to unlock the cargo doors."

"It's alright Mr. Wright. Sorry for any problems. We had a few complaints on this road. Take care of your wife. Be careful pulling out of here. You might want to stay here until the storm passes."

Chapter 5

With a little chill, and the sun peeking through the cotton wood trees at the eastern edge of the property near the chain-link fence, Russell with sweat running down his forehead, and dripping off the end of his nose, diligently packing the trunk of the Caprice.

Naomi looking around the nearly empty street, noticing the boys' running back and forth, and around the house apparently playing some kind of elusive game, yelling, "Denny, Anthony, calm down now. See if you can help your dad." Looking over and seeing Jacqueline standing in the middle of the empty asphalt street in the front of their house with thumb in mouth, two fingers up her nose, just watching the boys.

With hands on her hips Naomi yells "Jacquelyn, get out of the street."

Taking her thumb out of her mouth and her fingers out of her nose, "Mommy, me no in street."

"OK, little miss, stay up here near me."

Shutting the trunk looking up, "Alright. Everybody use the restroom. We won't be stopping for a while. I'd like to get as far as Biloxi by tonight."

"Jaki, Jackie, where are you?" called Naomi. Teetering up to the edge of the lawn and looking at her mother. "Let's put you in to those diapers I bought for you. Just for the trip. You can have your pretty panties as soon as we get to Houston" Naomi remarked.

Pulling her thumb out of her mouth and removing her fingers from her nose, "No Mommy. Me wear pretty panties."

"OK Jackie, but that means you have to act like a big girl."

Heading towards Highway 19, Naomi turned to Russell, "You know most people don't use 19 anymore."

"After all these years you must know my sense of direction. If I know how to get someplace I have to go that way every time. Maybe on the way back you can show me the new route. As of right now you are my official navigator. Just let me get out of Florida the way I know."

⁂

Looking at the dashboard clock, Naomi tapped Russ on the shoulder, "it's getting close to noon. I've packed lunchmeat and bread in the cooler. Whenever you find a rest area we can stop for lunch."

"I'd like to get as far as Pensacola." Opening and closing his hands. Holding the steering wheel with his left hand and them his right hand, shaking his hands, then glancing over to Naomi, "Think you could message my right hand? Feels like writer's cramp."

"You want me to take over for a while, maybe after lunch I could do a little driving?"

Breathing deeply, "I'm alright. Just need to get a little circulation in my hands. We'll see after lunch."

They found a picnic table among the sea oat and snow white sands of Ft. Walton Beach. "You know Russ I'll never get tired of the mounds of snow white sand and the sea oats."

"OK kids, there are public restrooms," pointing back toward the road, "over there. You better go now. I don't really want to stop until we get passed Biloxi."

⁂

From the back seat Denny is whining, "When we gonna stop?"

Naomi turning her head to the back seat, "Denny? We just stopped for lunch less than," looking at her wristwatch, "then an hour ago. Russ are we going to stop for the night?"

Russ was having a little problem as the sun was setting directly in front of him. Glancing over at Naomi, whose head was down on her chest and there was just a little drool on her chin, "Naomi, Naomi, I need my navigator."

Shaking her head wiping her mouth and rubbing her eyes, "What's the problem?"

"What else? I'm lost."

"Where are we?"

"Well, if I knew that I would have let you sleep. We just crossed the Alabama State line. Do you think you could find the air base? We really don't have to go on base. I just thought I'd take a look see."

"I can't say I can do much better, but this place does not look like the Biloxi we left. The only way I can find the base is by getting over on Highway 90, and then looking for White Avenue. I think I can find the main gate off U.S. 90. See you're really not much different than me. I also have to find something I'm familiar with. When did they put the casinos on the beach? I remember that little Mexican pizza place; guess it's gone."

"I tried to get us as close to the Air Force Base as possible. I can't believe how much the Air Force has changed since I enlisted. I guess everybody is trying to be politically correct. I'm not sure I like the new Air Force." Russ remarked.

❧

With the trunk open, and Russ putting their bags in the back. Looking over at Naomi, who was sitting in a chair in front of the Motel 6, skimming through the pages of a magazine, "Naomi, have I got all our bags?"

"I just put our clothes in the dryer."

"We haven't been on the road a full day. We already need to wash clothes?"

"I've already washed the clothes. They're in the dryer. And yes I needed to wash clothes. I'm not letting the grandparents see Jackie in a spaghetti stained outfit; it's her favorite outfit."

"O.K. that should be it? It is isn't it? Denny, go check the room make sure we haven't left anything behind?" Inquired Russ.

Coming out of the room with Jackie in her arms, "I think that should do it. By the way. Russ, I know how you are with your coffee. I think I saw a donut shop as we turned off the interstate."

With Naomi behind the wheel and within a few minutes they had stopped at a donut shop. The Gallagher's were once again on the road. The kids were already coming down off a sugar high.

Tapping Naomi on the shoulder, "Giving the kids donuts for breakfast may not have been one of our better ideas."

"Don't blame me for that."

"Well I didn't hear any objections from you." Naomi replied.

The closer they got to the state line the darker the skies got. Coming up on a bridge, Denny asked, "Daddy, is that the Mississippi River?"

"No Denny. I'm not sure, but once we cross the Mississippi we should be in Texas. We're crossing into Louisiana right now. That could be the Pearl River. No it's not. See that double span bridge. That's supposed to be the world's longest bridge. That's Lake Pontchartrain."

"Is that bridge longer than the Skyway?"

"Yes Denny. Most of the Skyway Bridge is causeway."

Tapping Russ on the shoulder, Denny asked "Are we gona stop for lunch?"

"Yeah. I saw a sign that claims that the best food in the South is at the next exit.

Which is five miles from here."

The sky was getting darker by the minute. It started with a light sprinkle, than a drizzle. As the rain drops get bigger Anthony leans over the seat, and tapping his father on the shoulder "I really have to pee."

The rain is now coming down in sheets, almost vertical. Leaning forward and squinting, Russ can barely see the exit sign. Less than a quarter mile off the highway Naomi spots what appears to be the restaurant. Pointing to the right she see tractor trailers, and at least a dozen cars.

Anthony practically climbing over the seat, he first grabs his mom than his dad, whining, "No. Not there. I promise I can hold it. Please we can't stop here."

Russ pulls the car off the road onto the shoulder just a few feet from the entrance to the restaurant. Everyone but Russ is staring at Anthony. "Why not Anthony? Why can't we stop here?"

"Because this is a bad place."

"Why is this a bad place, Anthony," Replied Russ.

Crying now, Anthony whines, "Something real bad is going to happen here."

"Well Antony we can stay in the car, but I have to stop. The rain is coming down so hard I can't see the road. I think maybe you just scared yourself."

Looking back at Anthony Naomi looks down, "Anthony did you just pee your pants?"

"I'm sorry momma."

"Well," once again looking down at Anthony's trousers, "We at least have to get you some dry pants and underpants."

Finding an open spot in front of the restaurant, Russell pulled in. unbuckling is seatbelt, turning and looking at his son, "I guess I've been delegated to taking Anthony in and getting him changed." Everyone including Jackie just stared at Anthony.

"You take Anthony into the restroom and we'll find us a table. "You want me to order you coffee?"

Anthony looking over at his mother, "That would be great."

"Not you Anthony. I was talking to your father. By the way are you still feeling bad about this place?"

"Yeah, I mean Yes mam. But I guess we, or I got us stuck here?"

"OK. I'll see you guys inside."

Walking into the restroom area Russ was assaulted by the odor of urine reminding him of a garbage strewn alleyway. Bending down and stiffing at Anthony's clothes Russ concluded that the smell was not all his sons'. Walking into the restroom Russ saw four toilet stalls and six urinals, and four rust stained sinks. Looking back at the door to make sure no one else was coming, Russ opened the bag that Naomi had given him with the change of clothes for Anthony.

There was no paper towels in the dispenser, but Anthony pointed to a trash can with a stack of paper towels sitting on top. Russ had Anthony take off his pants and underpants. Wetting several paper towels he helped Anthony wipe himself down. The door to the restroom squeaked. Russ looked up to see a large heavyset man start to enter. When the man saw Russ and Anthony, the surprised man commented, "Sorry," turned and left.

Russ called after him, "We'll be right out."

In contrast the dining area looked clean and neat. Naomi, Dennis and Jackie, who was already in a high chair were sitting at the far side of the doing room. Naomi spotted Russ and Anthony and waved them over to the table.

Anthony sat down next to his brother. Russ looked over at Naomi and holding the bag with Anthony's soiled clothes. "What do you think Anthony? You want to get something to eat here?"

Reluctantly Anthony replied, "Yeah, Yes sir. I guess." Holding the bag up, "I'll take these out to the car."

Russ is carrying something with him into the dining room it was a large pink diaper bag hanging over his shoulder. Handing the bag to Naomi, "I wasn't sure but I thought you might need this?"

Taking her thumb out of her mouth, and her fingers out of her nose, "Jackie no want diaper."

"Do you want your sippy cup?"

With her thumb back in her mouth, and shaking her head, Jackie replied, "Yeth."

"I would have completely forgotten about her sippy cup." Naomi replied reaching for the bag.

"Well did you guys order?"

"Daddy I want chicken tenders. I guess that answers my question. What about you Anthony. You want chicken tenders too?"

Looking up and taking a deep breath, "Can I get a chocolate milkshake?" Looking over at Jackie, Naomi asked, "What about you young lady. Do you want chicken tenders too?"

Shaking her head no, and pulling her thumb out of her mouth, "Jackie want fried cheese. Where my bunny?"

Naomi whipping Jackie's hands, "You mean you a grilled cheese sandwich? And I think I see your bunny sticking his head out of the bag. It **is** close enough to lunch time

"Well my dear I've heard you can eat breakfast anytime. Working shift work for most my working life I've been known to eat supper at six in the morning

Denny decided he would rather have sausage. Jackie had her pink bunny in one hand her brother Anthony's chicken strips in the other.

After her second cup of coffee. Looking at her daughter with her sippy cup upside down, "Let me take Jackie to the restroom where I can wipe her hands and let her go potty." Turning and looking toward the big picture window next to the register, "I think I actually see sunlight out there. It looks like the rain has stopped; at least for now."

Russ drained the last of his coffee, the boys were already standing, looking after their mother as she is headed for the ladies room, "We'll meet you in the car. By the way the men's was not that clean"

Standing next to the car Russ announces, "Last chance to use the bathroom." Denny looks over at Anthony, "We're alright. How much longer to Houston?"

"No more storms, and no traffic problems. We should be pulling onto Grandpa and Grandma's house in about four hours."

"**Nooo!**"That went right up Russell's spine, and the sound of a scream, "**MOMMY...MOMMY.**" Then silence.

The boys were looking at one another then their father, Denny spoke first, "Daddy. That was Jackie."

"Boys. Stay right here. Get in the car and lock the doors. Don't open the door until I get back."

Running and pushing the door to the ladies room open, Russ looks down to see his wife on the floor bleeding from her mouth, her hair matted with blood, and unconscious. Kneeling down beside her, the door to the ladies room opens the waitress that waited on them is standing above him. With her hands on her hips the waitress looks down at Russ, "What is going on here?"

I heard a scream, and found my wife laying here in a pool of her own blood. She was with my daughter."

Just then Naomi opened her eyes, and started to yell, "Where is my baby?" Looking at the waitress, "Please stay with her." He ran to the door and looked just in time to see a dark blue cargo van spitting up mud and gravel, sliding on the loose gravel and the wheels spitting more dirt, mud, and gravel as it fish tailed onto the highway.

Naomi was sitting up when Russ returned to the restroom. The waitress was just standing there staring at Naomi. Russ turned to the waitress, and in an authoritative voice, call the police and tell them this is an emergency."

A trooper was sitting across from Russ and the boys in a corner booth. Naomi was sitting at a chair across from the booth with an ice pack on her head. Looking up at Naomi the State Trooper asked, "Mam let me call the ambulance for you?"

Naomi started to shake her head, then moaned, "**Aweee!** No I can't go to the hospital. I need my baby."

The Trooper sitting in the booth with Russ and the boys and looking at Russ and then at Naomi, "I'm Senior Trooper Thibodeaux. Trooper Jackson is looking around the ladies room. Mrs. Gallagher you really should have someone look at that."

Russell's head was in his hands, his eyes were red and swollen. Anthony was crying, Denny was doing all he could do to keep from crying.

With effort Russell lifted his head and looked directly at the Senior Trooper, "I need to know what you are doing about getting our child back."

Thibodeaux looked over at Russell, Sir, I've radioed it in and there are people looking right now. Did you happen to notice a license plate?"

"Sorry. I know it was not a Louisiana tag."

Anthony looked up to see a State Trooper with Jackie's pink bunny in his hand. "Daddy, that's Jackie's bunny."

A tall thin black trooper walked up to Russ. Putting the hand with the stuffed rabbit out and handing it to Russ, "I'm Trooper Jackson; Greg Jackson. I found this on the floor." Looking over at Senior Trooper Thibodeaux. "I checked every stall, took pictures of the crime scene. I dusted what I could for prints; at least the flat surfaces. We're not going to get prints off the stuffed rabbit."

"Thank you Jackson. Did you radio the barracks?"

"Yes sir. They are calling headquarters and there will be a team sent out; including the forensic guys."

The Senior Trooper stood up and looked down at Russ, "Are you staying close by?"

Looking up and directly into the Senior Trooper's scat eyes, "No sir. We were on our way to Houston to visit with my folks."

"Thibodeaux looked over at the boys and then at Russ, We'll take it from here.

We need you guys to stay close. Do you have a cell phone?" Russell shook his head no.

Naomi replied, "I have a cell phone."

Thibodeaux continued, "Let me know where you will be staying. We'll call you as soon as we set up. We will set up near you and will be monitoring your phone. We will keep you informed of our progress, and as soon as we find something out we will tell you."

Naomi looked up at the Senior Trooper, and with red swollen eyes and a voice that sounded as if her sinuses where totally congested, "I am not leaving until you find my baby. I want my baby back right now." Her head was down, both her hands at her temples. It started with a mumble hardly heard by anyone, then there was a sound that seemed to come from deep within her. She stood up and reaching for the Senior Trooper she grabbed his collar, and started pounding on his chest, while yelling. "**NO, NO!** My baby is gone! I need you to do your job and bring my baby home. She continued pounding on the trooper's chest. Russ went to her and grabbed her shoulders, he then put his arms around her waist, and using all his strength he was finally able to pull her away from the Senior Trooper and through sheer force of will had her sit next to him.

Motioning to the waitress, Russ indicated that he wanted her to bring a glass of water.

Jackson turned to face Naomi, "We are doing everything we can. You can't stay here in this restaurant. There is a motel not far from here; it's very reasonable. Our Detectives are on their way. They're coming up from Baton Rouge; that's not that far away." Turning to the Senior Trooper, and then at the Gallagher's, Jackson in a low calm voice stated, "The FBI has been notified and they will also be here."

A tall man with a three day old gray growth of whiskers, wearing a stained apron walks over to Naomi, "Mam I am so very sorry. There is really nothing I can say, I've owned this place for over twenty years. We've had our share of rowdy customers. Been robbed couple times, but this has never happened before. At the same time Cheryl was motioning to Thibodaux, I've locked the doors put the close sign up."

"So ifen you need to stay a while it be alright with us. By the way I'm Karl." The man with the stained apron added.

Russell with red swollen eyes looked up at Karl, "I do appreciate all your kindness. "Ya know I was eaten sand and dodgen bullets for the last eighteen months, I really thought the worse was over. Karl, thank you and Cheryl for all your help."

Russell looked over at his wife. She was sitting at the edge of a cushioned seat the corner the booth, he noticed she had a weird look about her; she was just staring into space. Karl reached out a hand to Russell, and at that moment Naomi stood. As she was getting up, her hands came up to her temples and she fell flat on her face; not even trying to protect her face, landing directly on her nose; which was now bleeding profusely.

Trooper Jackson's eyes became round orbs as he reached for his radio. Looking over at the Senior Trooper, "I think we really need to get an ambulance here.

Two men banged on the door. Karl went to the door and examined their badges. Russell noticed it wasn't at all like the movies. They were both wearing Jeans the taller one had a sweat shirt on the short blond haired man was wearing a western shirt with a bolo tie with a turquoise and silver tie clip up near his throat.

Denny was the first to notice the reddish-brown cowboy boots on the shorter Detective. Looking down at the boots and then up at his father, "Daddy, I ain't never seen boots like that."

The short blond one with the cowboy boots just grinned at Denny then looked down on the floor at Naomi. Squatting down next to her reached down and helped her sit up. "Can you sit up? I mean do you feel like you are going to pass out again?"

Putting her hands back up at her temples, "I just have the mother of all headaches." She felt the blood from her nose going down her throat and she started coughing. Grabbing a handful of napkins, the Detective with the shiny boots handed them to Naomi, "Gently very gently blow your nose; Not too hard, you don't want to get the bleeding started again."

"Just lean back against the booth. We got a limousine coming for you."

Just as the Detective said that two men with a stretcher entered the door. Two more men entered. The shorter white haired man was wearing a brown suit with a subdued tie. The other man was tall, very tall, was in a charcoal suit with a red tie. Both had military style haircuts. Russell thought the shorter man's hair was almost as white as snow. The taller man's hair color was nondescript maybe a mousy brown or sandy. *What in the world am I thinking, my wife is laying on the floor with a bloody nose, my two boys look like zombies, and my daughter has been stolen, and I am trying to describe FBI agents?*

Trooper Jackson walked over to Russell, "If you'd like, you can follow the ambulance to the hospital. The Senior Trooper and I will brief the Detective and the agents. We all know where to find you."

The trip to the hospital was uneventful, except that if Russell had to find his way back to the restaurant. Russ could hear muffled crying of his two boys. Anthony, still holding the pink bunny rabbit tightly in his hand, leaned up against the front seat, "Daddy I am so sorry. We **will** get Jackie back."

Leaning is head back, "I know Anthony. We will. Now let's check on your mom." Naomi was taken into the emergency room where there were several people standing over her. The last thing Russell saw as they were escorting him out of the little room in the ER was a lot of shiny instruments near Naomi's nose. As he was leaving the room a woman in green scrubs entered with what looked like gauze and disinfectant.

Sitting in a chair in the hallway not far from the room that Naomi was in he saw a man with a gurney heading for Naomi's room. It just dawned on him that he didn't know where his boys where. Walking to the entrance to the ER, and looking through the small glazed windows he could make out his boys sitting on what looked like overstuffed couches watching TV.

He stood up as he saw the gurney with his wife on it pass him. Calling out to the two people in surgical gowns that were pushing the gurney, "Where are you taking her?"

The two men in suits with the white walled military style haircuts came up to Russ. The shorter of the two handed Russ a card, "I'm Special Agent in charge Asa Williams." Pointing to the man in the charcoal suit, "This is Special Agent Walton."

Two men in white lifted Naomi onto the gurney, and put her in the back of an ambulance.

Looking over at Russell's red swollen eyes, Special Agent Williams motioned for Russell to follow the ambulance, "Mr. Gallagher, it is Gallagher? You can follow the ambulance. We'll be along shortly."

A woman wearing white slacks, and a white blouse following the gurney turned to Russell and replied, "She should be fine. They want to get an MRI just to make sure there's no swelling on her brain, and to check for any other damage."

"Can I go down there with you?"

The nurse lifted her head, and turned to him, "Sure."

Chapter 6

Fishtailing out of the restaurant parking lot. Melvin looked over at Darlene. Her head was on her chest and she was drooling. He pulled the van off the road behind three Spanish moss draped oaks. Pulled behind some of the higher scrub bushes. He walked around to the cargo doors and very slowly and quietly open the cargo doors. He climbed up next to Jackie. He jerked her hair and with his big hands stroking her red locks. He seemed fascinated with her hair. She knew he was talking to her because she heard his voice, his words, but she couldn't distinguish anything coherent in them. She had stopped crying. She was now just whimpering. She could still hear him talking. She didn't want to listen to anything he had to say anyway. He was pulling at her panties. She was kicking and tried to scream. He put one hand over her mouth. She bit his little finger. He hit her with the back of his hand across her face. She was squirming, he was having trouble holding her hands still. He once again tried put his dirty hands over her mouth. This time she bit his thumb drawing blood. He pulled his hands away and with the back of his hand, he smacked her. For Jackie everything went black.

Just then Darlene woke, turning she yelled, "What's going on back there?"

Sliding out the cargo doors, "Just trying to get this kid to shut-up I think she was about to go into convulsions. I tried to restrain her but she bit me"

Melvin was now once again behind the steering wheel, "Darlene, will you shut that kid up."

47

Jackie was no longer crying or screaming; every rugged breath just caused her to whimper. Looking down at her purple face Darlene was sure the little girl was about to go into convulsions, and die. "Melvin what did you do to this baby?"

"I smacked her, and not that hard."

"Yes Melvin she has a bruise on her face. We better not let anyone see her."

The rain had stopped, but the windshield muddier than it was. Using the windshield wipers, and the mist spray just spread the mud over the windshield making it even harder to see. Melvin reminded Darlene of a dog hanging his head out of the window. In a shaky voice Darlene asked, again, "Melvin we have to wash the windshield."

"Can't stop until we cross the state line. Hey that kid is awful quiet. What did you do?"

"I still had a little Nyquil. She liked it. Ya know it taste like cherry syrup."

"**Damn!** Darlene she's just a baby. That could kill her. This kid is worth a lot of money. She ain't worth nutten if she's dead."

"I'm sorry Melvin, but she **is** sleepen."

"You just better hope that she wakes up."

Darlene squatting in the cargo area of the van taping Jackie on the shoulder. Getting frustrated, she shakes her. Jackie does not appear that she is going to wake up, "Wake up.

Wake up little one." Taking a deep breath, "**Melvin!** I can't get her to wake up. I think I killed her."

Still trying to see through the muddy windshield, Melvin yells back, "Darlene!"

"Is she breathing?"

"Yeah."

"Is her breathing deep and steady, or very light?"

"She's breathing deep and steady, but I can hear a rattle when she breathes"

"Well, just let her sleep. At least she has finally stopped her crying."

Climbing over the seat to sit next to Melvin, with a grunt and groan Darlene sits.

Turning to Melvin and pointing to a road sign, "Melvin that sign says we're heading toward Jackson. Isn't Jackson in Mississippi?"

"Yeah it is. We got to go this way to get home."

"Yeaa…But don't I…don't we have to go west. Last I checked Mississippi was east. "I know Darlene, but we got to go this way to get that way."

"Well we got to stop soon."

"Why? The gas gauge tells me we got more than half a tank. You got your medicine earlier."

"It's the kid. She stinks. I found a change of clothes in the diaper bag. We got to get someplace where I can clean her up."

Staring at Darlene, roaming onto the shoulder of the road, the tires spiting up gravel, Melvin turns abruptly almost losing control as the van slides kicking up gravel and dirt. "OK Darlene. I need to clean these windows…Aw, what is that smell?"

"I told you I need to clean the kid."

"Keep an eye open for Mile Marker 72. There should be restrooms there."

"I think she's waking up. Don't think she's going to be doing that much crying; maybe a little whimpering. She just says she wants Mr. Bunny."

"What the hell does that mean?"

"She keeps opening and closing her hands. I think it's some kind of stuffed animal. **Over there**."

"Over there what?"

"The mile marker and it looks like they got toilets."

"You need to find out her name. I mean people are going notice if we don't know what to call her."

Turning into the rest area, "Aw Shit!"

"What's the matter?"

"Unless it's Christmas those blue and red blinking lights mean cops. Just get back there with the kid, and keep her quiet. Melvin turns to his open window as the policeman walks up to his car standing at least two feet back from the door.

With his large flashlight the police officer bangs on the side of the van. "Sir would you please put your hands on the steering wheel?"

"Yes sir. What seems to be the problem?"

"Is there anyone else in the van?"

"Yes sir. My woman and kid are in the back. The kid has been complaining about a bellyache."

Walking up to the window the police officer steps away from the van and shines his light to the back of the van, "Mam could you lift up your hands, open your hands and turn your palms towards me?"

Darlene lifts up her hands, looks down at Jackie, "Honey, you just try and be quiet?

"Thank you mam. You can put your hands down. Sir using your right hand would you open the door, and step out?"

"Yes sir. Is there a problem?"

"Sir you seemed to having trouble keeping your van on the road. Would you come out here and take a little walk for me?"

"Yes sir. I got a bum leg."

"Well you can either walk the line for me or I can call the police van and have the paramedics take a little blood sample."

With a smile, and squinting against the reflection of the sun in the police officer's mirrored sunglasses, "Yes sir. I'll try walking for you."

Dark clouds started to cover the sun. Melvin feels droplets of water on his face. The wind picks up the rain is no longer a few droplets; it's starting to come down steady. Opening the door slowly, Melvin slides out of the van. Melvin walks away from the policeman than toward the policeman. His tee shirt is drenched. Melvin is starting to shiver as the wind picks up from the north. "Anything thing else officer?"

"One more thing lift up you right leg and put your finger on your nose." Melvin stood there with water starting to drip off his nose for what seemed like five minutes with his right leg up and his index finger on his nose; he was sure he was going to fall flat on his face. The sound of a crying child got both their attentions. With water starting to cascade off his wide brimmed hat, "I'm sorry sir but I followed you for about five miles and you seemed to be having trouble keeping your van on the road. I hear your child in there." Looking at the muddy windshield, "While you're here you need to wash that windshield. If you can see well enough to drive there is a gas station a couple miles down on the right side. Take the next exit and the gas station is just off to your right. No wonder you were having a problem keeping the van on the road. I'm going to give you a warning. As long as you keep your van on the road and stay within the speed limit you'll be OK. Now take care of that child. By the way is that a little boy or a little girl?"

"She sounds like she's got the croup, or somthen."

"Yeah, we need to get her home. Seems like she has a little congestion." The rain was now pouring off the brim of the officer's hat like a water fall.

"You say you've got a little girl back there? What's her name?"

"Her name is a…Sara, but she probably wouldn't recognize it. We've been calling her Snookum since before she was born."

Pushing his hat back and scratching his head, and holding his hat against the wind, with his head down against the wind the police officer climbed into his cruiser. Melvin could see the trooper pick up the mike. He put the mike back on the radio.

Leaning out the partially opened window he waved with his thumb up at Melvin. Rolled the window back up turned back to his steering wheel, turning off the lights, and pulled out onto the highway.

Opening the cargo doors Darlene stepped out with Jackie, Melvin cupped his hands against the wind and rain lit up a cigarette, inhaled deeply and let the smoke out slowly Halfway to the restrooms Darlene turned toward Melvin, "Are we gona be alright?"

"Yeah. I watched him on the radio. If he had a problem he wouldn't have pulled away and we would be seeing a lot more cops."

With the van's cargo doors open and holding Jackie in her arms Darlene was moving their camping gear, lifting up the sleeping bags, with the hand not holding the little girl ripping through her large hand bag. "Melvin get over hear, and hold this kid?"

She dumped the bag's contents on the floor of the van. "I can't find it?"

"You can't find what?"

"None of it."

"Darlene, what are you talking about?"

"The 'Scat'.

"You mean what we just scored?"

"Yeah, the 'scat', and the syringes. I talked to those people outside the Meth clinic. Somebody gave me a few syringes. Now they're gone."

"Darlene, did you just throw it out the door?"

"No, Melvin. It has to be that kid. Give her here. We definitely do not need her getten in my shit."

"Darlene your wrong. Larry has already advanced us several thousand dollars. We got to get the kid up to the house. You and I have a little work to do. We need to train her."

"Train her? What do you mean train her?"

"We got to get her to stop crying. Tell her that her mother is dead or somum."

"We can't do that. She's a little girl, and I don't know how much she knows."

"Well if I can train a puppy. I think the two of us can train one little girl."

"Melvin, when I train a dog I use a newspaper."

"Well we do the same thing with the kid. When she doesn't do what we want; just smack her with a rolled up newspaper. Let's try that and see if we can get her name."

"OK, Darlene We'll be coming up on a pretty good size city. I'm pretty sure we've got enough money to get your 'scat' there. I been here before. There's a sports bar not far from the exit. There used to be a dealer that would hang out there. I can't think of his name."

"When we stop for you to wash the windshield remind me to pick up a nice thick newspaper."

"Hey Darlene what do you feed a kid?"

Imagine she eats like any human being."

Looking into the setting sun, coming around the loop surrounding the city for the third time, Melvin irritated, and frustrated, glances over at Darlene, "I know where we need to go. I can see the neighborhood from here. What I don't know is how to get off this damn loop circling the city. I told you I'd take you to visit Elvis."

"Just take the first exit close to where you think we need to be."

"I see an exit. Who puts an exit on the left side of the road?"

At the next exit Melvin pulls the van off the road. Driving into an area of boarded up stores, and rundown empty tenements he sees black teenagers standing on a corner next to a store with windows so dirty that he couldn't tell if it was a store and if it was open. Might be just an old abandoned building.

Pulling over to the curb next to the building with the darkened dirty picture window a very large muscular black teenager wearing a long black trench coat walks up to the to the side of the van, "What you doen here?'

Melvin turned thinking, *it is hot out here and this kid is wearing a trench coat.* He turns toward the teenager, "Last time I was here there was a sports bat down here someplace.

The teenager reaches into one of the pockets of the trench coat. Melvin feels that familiar feeling in the pit of his stomach. The same feeling that kept him alive and making sure he was no one's bitch while in prison. The teenager brings his hand out of his pocket with a pack of cigarettes. Holding the pack out to Melvin. Melvin grabs one and while he is lighting the cigarette the teenager comes up with a knife in his hand. As the kid brings up the hand with the knife and strikes inside the open window, Melvin brings his hand down hard on the kid's wrist and in one motion brings his knife up and puts it through the kid's right hand, and casually pushes the knife midway in the kid's hand. The kid screams, but muffles the scream in a matter of seconds, the knife drops to the inside of the open window "Now as I was saying is that sports bar anywhere near here?"

With a very high pitched voice, for a very large boy, the kid replies, and "No sir." The kid looks down at his hand. "Please, please, pull your knife out of my hand." The kid tries to pull his hand, but manages to let out another yelp, "There was a bar like that but like everything else around here it be boarded up. Iffen you need weed or blow I can help."

"I want scat, I've been chasing the dragon for the last day. The word is I can get what I need here."

Melvin pulls the knife out of the kid's hand, then grabs his hand and with pressure holds it tight looking directly in the kid's dark brown bloodshot eyes, then looking down to see blood dripping from the kid's hand onto his pants. Pushing the kid's hand back. "I don't know kid. Is there anyone around here that can help me score Smack'?"

"All I got is blow, and weed."

"If you haven't noticed, I'm not all that pleased with you."

"Ya, yes sir I noticed. I'm going to reach in my pocket." Melvin gives him a stare, and let's go of his hand. "I'm just pullen out my phone. I know someone who can get you what you want. You got the green?"

The kid starts to turn, Melvin pops the door of the van open and grabs the kid's wrist. "You callen your supplier?"

"Yes sir."

"You can stay right here while you call."

"The man don't like meeten new people."

"Well you just tell him if he wants the sale he'll meet me here."

"How do I know you ain't the man?"

"Well you don't. But, if you don't get me what I want your momma ain't even goin a recognize you."

The kid rubbing his hand, and looking to his right and his left. Looking for his bros, and seeing the street empty. "OK."

Melvin looked back down the deserted street to see a short skinny old black man with short cropped gray hair, wearing clean pressed khakis, and a blue striped tee shirt walking towards him. As the man approach and looked directly at him, Melvin looked down to see that the man was wearing sandals, "You the one that took me away from the ballgame? Open your shirt. Now come closer. Drop your pants."

Melvin reached for his belt. Then looking over at the old black man, "I bet you're not even going to take me out to dinner? "

"Pull you pants up. I don't need to see your junk. Now what do you want?"

"I need brown, snow or whatever in other words like I told your boy here, I need to make a buy."

"Not much tonight, maybe just little more than a taste, but I'll have more tomorrow. Now let me see the green."

Melvin opened his hands, I'm goen a reach in my pocket. He pulled out a roll of bills. "Ya know I been thinken. Maybe I need to go someplace else to get what I need?"

"If you got the green?" looking at the wad in Melvin's hand, "I can maybe get you a tenth of a gram."

"OK. Here's the deal. You sell me a gram, I'll give you a C note."

"You got it with you? You willin to pay that much?" The black man shook his head. "OK. You got a sale."

Digging in his pocket the old man pulls out two square shaped aluminum foil packets.

Melvin turned to his van and carefully opened the two packets put the powder on a wet index finger tasted it, refolded the packets, "Thank you sir it has been a pleasure doing business with you."

Climbing back in the van, Melvin looked back into the cargo area. Seeing, more like hearing Darlene and the kid taking turns snoring.

He did notice a little whimper, almost like a puppy, out of the little girl. The heat was becoming oppressive.

Darlene was climbing over the seat as he made an exit onto the highway. Putting her face next to the air conditioning vent, with a sigh and fanning herself with the rolled up newspaper, "Where are we going now?"

Handing Darlene two squared aluminum wrapped packets. "You got any syringes? She shook her head. "Darlene, we are going home." Pointing to the packets in her hand, "That had better last." The sky was getting darker, the drizzle had turned to rain. Thunder could be heard in the distance. The wind was now once more coming in from the north; becoming colder.

Crossing into the Dakotas, the sky was even darker. They had driven out of the heavy rain, but the light drizzle was freezing on the windshield. Melvin turned on the heat. He spotted the lights of a dinner coming up on the left side of the single lane blacktop. Yelling, "Darlene waky waky. Come on Darlene wake up. I gotta get some coffee, maybe even somthen to eat."

Sitting in a booth at the far corner of the truck stop dining room, Darlene glanced over at Melvin. "Think I want a cheese burger. Think the kid will eat a cheese burger?"

"Don't know what little rug rats eat. Heard they've been known to eat crayons."

"No Melvin. We are not feeding the kid crayons."

A sound, more a mumble from the kid. Darlene looked over at Melvin, "Did you hear that?"

This time it was clear, "Jackie want hamburger."

"OK. **Now** we know how to get the kid to behave." Replied Melvin.

Melvin just shook his head as he stared at Jackie. The hamburger bun in pieces on the highchair tray, her mouth, already full and chomping steadily.

Darlene knew the Black Hills were close, but they were hidden by dark clouds and rain. The windshield wipers were on the high setting. The rain was so thick at times that the van's headlights just reflected the light making the road almost impossible to see.

They had been driving for a few hours, and getting close to home. The rain had all but stopped. Light snow flurries were now taking the place of rain. The sky lit up with a strike of lightning and a crash of thunder. The snow flurries were now large snowflakes. Melvin seemed to be hitting puddles and pot holes on the narrow street. Passing boarded up store fronts, and finally turning onto an icy snow covered road. Melvin could barely see his double wide. The snow drift in front of the trailer was at least five feet deep. Melvin knew there was a driveway. There were also drainage ditches near the side of the road; the ditch and the driveway were covered in snow. Melvin got out of the van, worked his way to the back, and using the shovel they had found in Louisiana, wandered the front lawn like a blind man with a white cane. After finding the driveway he cleared enough snow to see worn tracks of the driveway. After slipping and sliding he finally managed to get onto the driveway and close to the trailer.

Darlene sliding out of the back of the cargo van reaching back to pick up her hand bag and Jackie. Jackie's head flopped to the side as Darlene picked her up. "Melvin this child is burning up." Jacquelyn made a little grunt as Darlene walked towards the double wide. Turning back towards Melvin, "Someone tacked an envelope to the door."

Yelling from the van, "What does it say?"

"It's too dark and way too cold. I can't even feel my fingers."

Trying to balance Jackie in one arm and insert the key with the other hand. Stooping down and squinting and then putting her frozen fingers on the lock. Trying again to insert the key, "Melvin, I can't get the key in the lock. Would you shine your flashlight on the lock?"

Shining the flash light on the door lock, "Does that help?"

"I think the lock is frozen."

"OK. You and the kid get back in the van. I'll see if I can heat up the lock; which can actually sometimes make it worse."

Climbing in the back of the van Jackie is sweating and shaking. Darlene wrapped her in one of the blankets in the back of the van and put her in a sleeping bag. Jackie looks up at Darlene and vomits. "Oh shit. How gross." Was Darlene's response.

Trying to jiggle the key into the lock, afraid to twist the key too hard. *All I need now is to break the key off in the lock.* "What's a matter Darlene?"

"Oh Melvin, the kid just puked all over me."

"Woo."

"Woo? I just said the kid puke all over me."

"I got the door open. The lights seem to be working. I'll turn the water heater up. You can clean up."

Putting Jackie on the couch, looking over at the kitchen table at the envelope. "Well Melvin are you going to open the envelope?"

"Yeah. Let me get the circulation back in my hands."

"Here give it here." Tearing the envelope open several bills fell on the floor, "Somebody left us some money."

"Must be from Larry. He wasn't supposed to be here until tomorrow. Darlene you read the note; the feeling is just coming back in my hands." Handing the note to Darlene.

"Says he was early and was hoping the package was ready for shipping. It's signed Labeeb. What's Labeeb?"

"That's Larry. I just feel funny calling him Labeeb."

Undressing Jackie Darlene notices that her skin is almost blue, there seems to be a rash all over her body. When she breathes she can hear a gurgling and a squeaky wheezing sound coming from Jackie. "Melvin, this child is so hot it feels as if she is going to burn my hands."

"Well we don't have any aspirin. Get her in the shower and run the cold water."

"Then what?"

"While you're cleaning you and her up I'll start the van. We're taking her to the hospital."

"The clinic's closed. The ambulance with the EMTs should be there, but she needs a doctor."

"I know that. I said we were taking her to the hospital. I don't think Larry can pay me enough for this."

Chapter 7

Naomi was being hustled, first to ex-ray. Where she was put in a tunnel. More waiting. She was taken into a small examining room where a small section of her head was shaved and a nurse put sutures in that small shaved portion of her head. The wound was deep and it took three stitches. Russ and Naomi waited in another small room, Naomi lying back on an examining table. Finally a man identifying himself as Doctor Abadi. "I would like very much to," Looking down at Naomi, "Have you stay here for the night." Naomi, sitting up just stared at the doctor. "Very well. It looks as if you bruised your nose, the nose is not broken; however you will probably wake with two black eyes. From, what I can see there is no swelling, except for your nose. I have no doubt you have a mild concussion. When you get home put a cold compress on you face, just your eyes and nose. I'll prescribe a mild pain reliever. I think I will give you a mild sedative. You must wait until you get home to take the sedative. I would also like for you to stay awake for a while, so wait for at least an hour before you take the sedative. You are not driving are you?"

Russell looked out into the waiting area to check on his boys, "Doctor I am now confused. First you tell me to give her a sedative when we get home. Now you say to wait an hour and keep her awake."

Rubbing his eyes, the doctor replied, "Yes that is correct."

Shaking his head, helping Naomi off the examining table, and motioning to the boys to follow him. With a sigh, Russell gestured for the boys to come over and help him get their mother in the car. Helping Naomi bend her head down. "Naomi watch your head."

Just as Russell was about to climb into his car, his heart felt as if it would stop as he felt a tap on his shoulder. Turning abruptly he saw the FBI agent with the snow white hair was actually slightly shorter than Russell, with white hair that reminded Russ, that if it weren't for his ruddy complexion would look like his son Anthony. "You scared the shit out of me."

"Sorry." Handing his card to Russ, "We met at the restaurant. My partner, Special Agent Walton and I walked in as your wife was being carried out on a stretcher."

"I really didn't notice much."

Rubbing his jaw, "Well I am Agent Asa Williams, and the Agent in charge. We, Agent Walton and I were just about to ask a few questions when they carried your wife to the hospital. First let me tell you how sorry I am about what you have been through. The troopers gave us a very good report, so I won't ask you to go through it again, unless you can think of anything else. I would like to ask your wife a few more questions. It would be better if I could do it now, but I don't think she is in any shape right now. So I would like to come by in the morning."

"I don't even know where I'll be in the morning."

"We presumed to arrange two rooms for you in the motel across the street from the restaurant. Our friendly federal government will cover your expenses." Looking up at Russ, "You do know I am being sarcastic? Anyway I'd appreciate you not tell my supervisors as they really lack a sense of humor. Anyway I'll give you a call in the morning."

Looking into the car and then at the agent, "Agent…"

Looking up at Russ, "I know you weren't expecting to be staying here. If there is anything else I can do for you please let me know."

"I really have to get my wife and kids someplace to rest."

"If you were wondering, we have a very good working relationship with the State and local authorities."

"Where is this motel?"

"Right across the street from the restaurant." Scratching his head, "Sorry. Just follow me."

"Detective. I don't know how much sleep any of us will get, but could you at least wait until the sun rises?"

"Yes sir. Speaking of getting in touch. Do you happen to have a cellular phone?"

"No but my wife does."

The street lights were giving Russ a headache. The drive back to the highway didn't really take that long.

Watching the Detective enter the office, *'I wonder how tall he really is without the boots?'*

Russell's head was back on the seat rest when Agent Asa Williams tapped on the window of the car, "Mr. Gallagher, could I borrow your wife's phone. It will only take a few minutes. Your rooms are on the second floor." Russ put his hand out to retrieve the keys to their rooms, looking up he noticed a Navy blue, full-sized van slow and then park next to the office of the Sun Downer Motel in Slidell Louisiana. Four men, dressed in different navy-blue polo shirts, tan tactical pants, and combat boots, sat inside the van. With practiced expertise, the burly men with crew cuts set up a small dish antenna.

Asa looked over at is partner and with his hands motioned that he would be a few minutes longer. "Mr. Gallagher, that van has listening devices in it. We will be monitoring your cell phone. You may not believe this now but that van will become unobtrusive once they are completely set up."

"Yes I do believe you. I've spent many hours in the Syrian Desert doing the very same thing."

"Well that van belongs to the FBI. Those four burly men with crew cuts belong to the FBI. Give me a few minutes with your phone. I'll bring it back to you shortly."

While Agent Williams was going over o the van, Russ was trying to help his wife up the stairs to their rooms. The first couple steps went well but Naomi started to stagger. She almost fell when Agent Walton appeared to catch her.

"Hey dad me and Anthony have our own room."

Helping Naomi to one of the two large queen sized beds, "Look again boys. There's a door that opens right into my room. We will keep that door open."

Reaching into her purse, Naomi pulls out Jackie's pink bunny and places it on the dresser, "Oh Russ what am I going to do. Strangers have got my baby."

"From the looks of things they have all the law enforcement agencies here in the parking lot."

Just then Anthony came running into the room, "Daddy I am sorry. We will get Jackie back I promise."

Plopping down on the other bed, beckoning for Anthony, "Anthony it is not your fault, but you are right we will get Jackie back."

It really wasn't that hot, as a matter of fact it was getting cool if not cold outside. Russell heard the heat kick on. He was lying on the other queen size bed alone. He had the sheets pulled down but he was in his underwear on top of the sheets with his arm across his eyes listening to his wife's moans, and deep breathing in the other bed.

He may have dozed off for a few minutes. The sun was coming through the blinds. Naomi was standing by the window with what looked like a small glass of iced tea. He threw his legs on the floor before sitting up. On standing he walked over to his wife. Putting a hand on her shoulder, "Where did you get the iced tea?" as he moved up closer he realized it was not iced tea. He could smell the booze. Where did you get the booze?"

While you were asleep I went down to the office and asked the night clerk where I could get a drink. He told me to wait." She took a large swallow of the amber beverage. "I don't know where he went, but he was gone for about five minutes and sold me this." Holding up a pint size bottle.

"Whiskey?"

Turning back to the window holding one of the blinds up and peering outside at the parking lot, "No Russ it's actually bourbon. I was going to buy a coke, but the machine is right outside our door; thought it would make too much noise, and I didn't want to wake you. I started with a little ice and water. I still have ice and I don't need any more water."

Looking over at the dresser and seeing Jackie's pink bunny. Naomi walked over to the dresser and picked up the stuffed bunny. Put her face on the bunny and sniffed, then started to cry. Between sobs, "You know Russ I thought the bourbon might numb me or at least let me sleep; no such luck."

Putting his arms around her, "Naomi is that going to help your headache?"

Walking back to the window, "Russell, I don't know, but I thought the numbness might help." She replied.

Pulling one of the blinds up and looking out at the parking lot, Russ spots the van that Agent Williams told him about. Putting his arm around Naomi and pointing through the blinds, "That van over there is a listening post set up by the FBI. You know I really don't think it's a good idea to drink that after taking the sedative the doc gave you."

Naomi pushing her hair back away from her face, "I need very much to take a shower; probably a cold shower. Would you check on the boys?"

"I will check on our boys. That Agent Williams said he is coming up here sometime this morning. That reminds me I lifted your cell phone out of your purse. It's on the dresser. He said he would call before he came up. So don't take too long in the shower."

When Naomi came out of the shower in her robe with a towel wrapped around her head, Russ reached into his toiletries bag took out a small bottle of mouth wash and handed it to his wife. "Make sure you brush your teeth and rinse."

Russ and Naomi were dressed, Naomi in dark slacks and a light pink blouse. Russ put on his faded jeans and a brown tee shirt. The boys were in shorts and sweat shirts sitting on the floor in front of their parents watching TV, or pretending to be watching the television when there was a knock on the door. Russ opened the door and looked down to see Agent Asa Williams, the sun reflecting off his snow white hair. "Agent I thought you were going to call?"

"Mr. Gallagher I did call but my call went right to voice mail."

Russ picked up the cell phone and looking over at his wife, "Naomi what does this mean. I pressed the button and your phone seems to be dead."

"It means I forgot to charge it."

Pushing his hair back, "Agent I am so sorry. Please come in. Boys go over to your room." Sitting on the edge of the bed Naomi looked over and motioned for Russ to pull the straight backed queens chair over for the detective."

Pulling the straight back chair away from the window, "Please sit."

Agent Williams had a small recorder in his hand. "Mr., Mrs. Gallagher, do you mind if I record our conversation?"

Russ shook his head, Naomi relied. "No."

Taking a breath and looking over at the Gallagher's, and laying the recorder on the arm of the straight back chair he was sitting in. "First let me assure you that as soon as the troopers called in an abducted child, road blocks were set up and a search parties were being formed. You gave a photo of your daughter to the trooper. He sent it out as soon as you gave it to him."

Naomi was having a problem sitting on the edge of the bed.

Asa continued, "The FBI resources that are available include Special Agents to assist in Interviews, Neighborhood Canvassing, Road Blocks, Evidence Response teams, and a computer forensics and response teams. Normally they take the lead. We are teamed as equals with the Louisiana State Police."

Agent Williams repeated many of the questions already asked. Naomi was asked several times during the interrogation if she could give a description of the person the knocked her out.

"You said you were digging through the diaper bag?"

"Yes."

"Before you were knocked out what did you see?"

"I felt someone tugging at the diaper bag. I smelled dead fish, turned to look up and briefly saw what looked like a fair skinned Mexican, with unkempt mousy brown short hair. I did notice yellowed teeth. Oh yeah. I don't think I'll forget the smell of her breath. I don't know which was worse, my babies dirty panties or the smell of that woman's breath."

Looking at Russ, "What made you stop at this particular restaurant?"

"We were hungry, plus Jacquelyn was not the only one that needed cleaning up." Pausing the recorder, the detective ask if he could get a drink of water. Russ put some of the left over ice in glass and filled it with water handing the glass to the detective. Turning the recorder back on, "You said she was not the only one that needed to get cleaned up?"

"Yeah, Anthony had a small accident. He said he had to go pee. I don't think we stopped soon enough. Then he said not here, please not here."

"Russ. Do you mind if I call you Russ?"

"No."

"Did you tell anyone that you would be or might be stopping at this particular restaurant?"

Russ was thinking the only thing missing was that table with the bare light bulb above it. The Agent was sipping water from the glass which made Russ think how much he would like a coke or just a cool glass of water. Several hours passed when Agent Asa Williams left.

"Boy he didn't leave anytime too soon. I really have to pee."

Naomi let out a sigh and then took a deep breath. "Don't take too long. I'm next." Coming out of the restroom, "Did you do whatever you had to do to get that phone working?"

Skipping to the bathroom, "Yes Russell I recharged it."

He could feel eyes on his back. Turning he could see the boys staring at him. "OK boys what is it?"

Denny spoke up, "Just wondering...Think we could get a hamburger or sompum?"

"Naomi, if we go across the street to the diner do we have to check in with the people in the van?"

"They can always reach me on my phone. Plus we are only going across the street.

Just as the four of them were about to go out the door, Russ literally ran into Agent Williams, "Oops. Sorry bout that. We were just heading down to the restaurant. My kids are like those birds you see with their mouths open."

"I was just coming up to see if I could borrow a piece of clothing that Jackie recently wore; preferably one that hasn't been washed. We are sure or suspects were at Honey Island. I'd like to use Jackie's clothing to let the dogs get a sniff. The video I saw has a stamp date well before your child was abducted. I don't think they will find anything in that swamp.'

That place across the street puts out a good breakfast I've heard that they have best beignets in all of Louisiana." Scratching his short white hair, "Yeah you should still have time for breakfast." Looking over at Naomi's raised eyebrows. "Oh beignet is like a donut, but I'm sure they are a lot more fattening; or so I've been told" Looking at Russ then at Naomi, "I really don't think either of you have anything to worry about."

Anthony ran out the door and right into Agent Williams. "Sorry."

"Seems like me running into your family is becoming a habit."

Tugging on Russell's pant leg, "But daddy you just got to listen to me."

Denny chimed in, "Yeah Daddy please listen to Anthony."

Traffic was light. Looking both ways Russ gabbed the boys and ran across the street, Naomi was trailing behind.

Entering the restaurant Anthony was still trying to tell his dad abut Jackie. "Dad you just got to listen."

Denny putting his hand on his brother's head, "Dad please at least tell someone."

"I promise as soon as Agent Williams comes back I'll tell him what Anthony said." There was a little crowd on entering the restaurant. Russ had smack right into a wheel chair. In the wheelchair was perhaps the oldest man he had ever seen; even older than the old Bedouin sheep herder he met in the Syrian Desert. This man's face was sallow and covered with an incredible tracery of wrinkles; bony white knuckles that grasped the arms of the chair almost threatened to burst through the tissue-paper skin. Extreme age had shrunk and twisted his body into the shape of a comma. There was a large man with a belly that threatened to bust out of his bib overalls. With red swollen eyes He bent over the wheel chair and whispered something in the old-man's ear. Looking first at Russell and then at Naomi, "This here is my paw-paw, Mr. Boudreaux. I'm Kyle Renee Boudreaux"

Mr. Boudreaux raised a shaky hand and covered Naomi's hand, the old man spoke, barely audible, and with the sound of the oxygen tank on the rear of the chair, "Como sava?"

Kyle spoke up, "My Paw-paw ask how's it going."

"Well sir we have had better days, as a matter of fact I know I have had better weeks." Replied Russ.

Putting slight pressure on her hand, looking up with the clearest blue eyes Mr. Boudreaux, whispered, "Listen to the boy."

Chapter 8

A twenty-one mile drive up to Crow Agency Montana should have taken half an hour, but with the blowing snow and icy winds they had already been on the road for over an hour.

They found Hospital Drive. The hospital appeared dark. The snow in the parking lot was deep. "Melvin, I don't think anybody is here. Look its dark at the hospital and I don't see any cars in the parking lot."

"It's a hospital Darlene. There has got to be somebody here."

Jackie's fever was still high. She was starting to stiffen in Darlene's arms. They fought their way to the doors. Melvin pulled on the door it didn't budge. Looking at Darlene, and yelling, tying to be heard over the howling wind, "What do we do now?"

Just then out of the corner of Darlene's eye she spotted movement. A man with a thick lamb skin coat pushed the doors open. "Come in. get out of the cold." Once inside the heat hit Darlene, taking her breath away, "Please, my baby is sick."

Melvin Wright stared at the female desk clerk, waiting until she finished her telephone conversation. Her name was Karen, and she was very pretty. She was also having problems with the computer on her small desk.

The girl at the desk finally got off the phoned and motioned for them to come up to the desk. "You do know we are not excepting patients. I can have our ER doctor look at her."

"Darlene, I had not thought of that"

Slowly getting up off the chairs in the lobby, "Thought of what Melvin?"

"Computers. That's all we need is for our names to pop up somewhere. Believe me they are already looking for us."

"Melvin the way she is banging on that computer, I don't think its working."

"That may be Darlene, but to get the kid in here I'm going to have to show them my tribal identification. When that computer gets back up we are in deep shit. She just said they are not taking patients."

"Well Melvin, I don't think they are looking for me. I still have my tribal Identification. Remember my last name is Prescott."

Although it did not look like anyone was at the hospital. Melvin thought it was one of the janitors that opened the doors for him. Wandering around the desk, he noticed that there was some activity in the back.

Karen, the pretty girl at the desk picked up the phone, Melvin was sure she was going to sound some kind of alert. She actually push a button on the phone, "Could Nurse Runningdeer come to the admitting desk?"

A square shaped woman wearing her black hair in a single braid, wearing white slacks, and white smock, with a blue sweater came into the lobby. Looking over at Darlene, "Is that the baby with a problem? Motioning for Darlene to follow her, "Follow me the doctor is waiting for her."

Melvin couldn't help staring at the nurse. The only time Melvin remembered seeing a Crow woman in braids was at a Pow Wow.

Calling after Darlene, "I'll just wait here."

Nurse Running Deer looking back at him, "You can come. The doctor is on his way. We just need to get this little thing comfortable.

While Darlene watched Nurse Running Deer lift Jackie onto a gurney and motioning for her to follow, Melvin patted his shirt looking for his cigarettes. Finding a partially crushed pack of smokes he went out the entrance. Standing at the edge of the driveway, he sensed a presence of someone. There was a shadow at the corner of his eye. For a second it felt as if his heart would stop. The reflection of the entry light eliminated a bear of a man with a pink puckered scar on his left cheek. He was wearing a lambskin coat. As the man turned to face him, Melvin caught the sparkle of a badge. "Sorry. I know I shouldn't but I really needed a smoke."

Looking directly into Melvin's eyes, "I haven't seen you before. Where are you from brother?"

"Me. That is my woman and little girl got us a place down in Lodge Grass. The baby is pretty sick. That's why I drove up here. We only got a clinic down there and it ain't open at night."

Melvin notices the tribal policeman's large, brown, scared, and callused hands as he pulled is gloves off, "I am Sam White Horse. We try to send a patrol down that way when we can. Its real hard on a night like this." Sam White Horse pulled the ear flaps up on his fleece line hat. Taking his hat off the light from the door caught the puckers pink scar on Sam's left cheek. The scare seemed to run from the deep laugh lines around his eye almost to his chin. Pulling his fleece hat off Melvin notices that the policeman is wearing his hair long; it comes down almost to his waist. He turned to enter the hospital. Looking over his shoulder, "You never told me your name."

Melvin called over to the tribal policeman, "I am Melvin, and I just need to get some of this smoke in my lungs. I'll be right behind you."

Sam White Horse pulled one of the folding chairs in front of Karen's small desk. Karen had her back turned to him filing the recent admission forms. Smacking his snow covered hat against his knee. Startled Karen, and she turned abruptly to see the policeman. "I am so sorry Sam. You really have to start making some noise when you come in."

Scooting the chair closer to her desk, "I did. Didn't you hear me smack my hat against my knee? Could I get a look at your most recent admission? By the way I thought you weren't admitting patients."

"That is true, but the child that just came in will not make it to Billings. Nurse Running Deer says she needs to be stable before she can be transported."

Leafing through the thin file. He looked up at Karen. "Says here that a Jackie Prescott was admitted. It has Darlene Prescott as her guardian. I don't see a man's name?"

"No, the woman said that the child, Jackie Prescott was actually her cousin's kid. She was just watching her while the cousin went away for a while."

Picking up the registration form and pursuing the form looking for name date of birth and address. Thanks." Handing the file back to Karen, "What is the cousin's name?"

"Sam, I do not know. The little girl started going into convulsions. I called Kate to take her back. Never got a chance to finish the form."

"Something ain't right. That is a little white girl. I mean freckles and red hair?"

"Sam, my sister lives in Billings. She married a white, and two of her kids have a complexion like cream. I haven't seen them in a while, but I think the youngest has red hair" Starting to get up, Sam stopped and turned back toward Karen, "Did you use the computer. I mean did you transmit that information to Public Health?"

"No Sam the computers are down. I thought I would get the rest of the information later."

Sam heard the static from his radio. "Sam you there?"

"Yeah boss I am still here."

"OK wise guy. What is your twenty?"

"I am at the hospital thawing out. Got a bad feeling. There is a stranger here. Got a funny feeling about him. From what I can tell he and his woman brought in a little white girl."

"Well if we ain't got any wants or warrants just let it alone. Give me a name. As soon as the computer comes up I'll check on your stranger. I am surprised the radios are working."

"I am going to grab some of that hot stale coffee they have here. Know what I just figured? Over."

"What is that Sam?"

"Ya know the four wheel drive on these SUVs ain't worth a healthy shit on this ice."

"Ten-four. Be careful out there."

Just as Sam was filling a paper cup with hot coffee a middle aged woman with unkempt mousey brown hair came running out of the ER screaming, and breathing as if she was having trouble catching her breath. "Aweee! There's a ghost in there. There's a ghost in there."

Darlene stopped in front of the bear called Sam. "Officer there is a ghost in there." Melvin was just inches behind Darlene, "Darlene, calm down." As Melvin tried to hold her. She shook him off her, like a dog shaking water off.

Sam came over to Melvin and Darlene. Darlene was completely incoherent. Melvin spoke up. "Officer I don't know what that is about."

Nurse Kate Running Deer followed close behind, with a stuffed pink bunny in her hand. "Mam. That little girl is supposed to be in a sterile environment. I'm sorry but you just can't leave," with the stuffed bunny in her hand, "this in the oxygen tent with her."

Sam tried to lightly touch Darlene. She shook his hand off her shoulder. Walking towards the entrance, turning back to Melvin, "Melvin I got to get out of here."

The policeman just stared at Darlene and Melvin. "Don't you want to be here with the little girl?"

Melvin spoke, "We are not going far. Darlene is just very tired. I am sure once she calms down she will be able to go back in there with the baby."

Nurse Running Deer had been standing off to the side, "Sam. It's Ok. The little girl's fever has broken, and she is now sleeping. We have monitors on her. She is now being given antibiotics. She had to be intubated." Responding to Sam's unasked question, "We are assisting her breathing. She is in an induced coma."

Melvin hesitated for a brief minute and then moved up to listen to the conversation. Looking up at the policeman, "I'm sorry. Excuse me."

Answering Sam's unasked question, "Unlike the more typical way of being intubated or put on a breathing tube in their mouth, this child has the ventilator tube in her nose." Raising an eyebrow, "A ventilator is necessary for very young children. Poor thing has wires on her chest to monitor temperature and a probe to help regulate her temperature and probes to monitor her heart rate and respiratory or breathing rate. On top of that there is an IV in her belly button. Plus all this we need to keep her hydrated, so she is being given fluids. You know Sam if I hadn't been doing this for a very long time, after seeing my baby with all those tubes and needles I would probably like to run out of here too, but then again I couldn't leave her not for a second."

Melvin nodded toward the nurse, "I'm going to see how Darlene is doing. You know I'm sure she is concerned."

Looking at Melvin, "I understand the child is not yours?" asked Nurse Deer.

"That's true." Melvin replied. "Is she going to be alright? Is she gona be alright?"

Starting to walk back toward the small cubical where they had Jackie, "Mr. Prescott, we will do all we can. She really is in bad shape. It is a good thing you got her in when you did. I don't suppose you have her health history, or her shot records, you know immunizations' she may have had?"

Melvin was starting to sweat, "I'll check with Darlene."

Once outside Melvin came up behind Darlene, turned her towards him. "Listen Darlene we got to get out of here. That cop is asking a lot of questions."

"What about your friend, Larry?"

"He's not gona want the product now. He may want his money back. We'll take care of that whenever."

Climbing into the van Melvin literally grabbed Darlene by her arms and pulled her into the van.

"Melvin we just can't leave the baby here."

"Why not? She is being taken care of. Besides I don't think we are going to get the rest of our money anyway. I mean the package is damaged."

Looking back at the door to the hospital, hoping that the policeman wasn't watching him. "You know Darlene, Larry may not want her, but I know somebody who would pay a lot for a little girl like that."

"What are you saying?"

"I'm saying there are a lot of men out there that would pay a pretty penny for something so young, and pretty."

"What are you saying Melvin?"

Melvin just glared at her, "Darlene we made a deal with a very dangerous man. That little girl was going someplace where they have a lot of little girls. Probably someplace in the Middle East."

"You mean she was going to be somebody's property?"

"Come on Darlene. We need to get out of here. There's something weird about that cop."

Darlene slammed against the door of the van as it went fishtailing out of the parking lot. "Take it easy, Melvin. I just barely got the door shut."

Stepping out the front door of the hospital Sam looked up to see a blue van fishtail out of the parking lot. He tried to get a look at the license plate; it was dark and too far away. The one thing came to Sam's mind. *That has to be Melvin and his woman. Why are they leaving that baby?*

Clicking her seatbelt, Darlene looked down to see a pink stuffed bunny ear sticking out of the bag she called her purse. "Melvin we have to go back."

"What do you mean we have to go back?"

"I've got the baby's stuffed bunny. She'll want it when she wakes up."

With his hands tight on the steering wheel. "Darlene, I was getting that feeling. I have a bad feeling. We need to get as far away as possible."

"Are we going back to our place?"

"Only for a few minutes. We need to get a few things then hit the road." Patting Darlene on her knee, "We'll be at our place real soon. Just keep your eyes open. Let me know if you see anyone, cars people, anything."

With wheels spinning and the van fishtailing they finally pulled into their drive. Melvin did not turn the engine off right away. He didn't see anyone. Whatever tracks they had left earlier were covered by fresh snow. His heart felt as if it dropped to the pit of his stomach when he noticed the front door to the trailer was open; just slamming back and forth in the wind, and the lights in the kitchen were on he turned the light of the van off, and coasted closer to the double wide "Darlene did you lock the door?"

"I don't remember."

"What about the lights?"

"Melvin I can't remember. We were in a hurry to get the kid to the hospital."

"Darlene stay right here. Let me take a little look."

Creeping up on his own crib. He avoided the open door and snuck up to the kitchen window. The window was a little high even for him. He found an old plastic milk crate; he had used to transport his extensive video collection. He stood on it and looked through the window. It seemed empty. He went around to the back window. There was no sign of activity. Brushing ice and snow off his trousers and pulling his gloves off, he went to the van, "Darlene, if somebody was here they are gone now. You need to get your bag, and pack some stuff you might need. I'll do the same."

The last of the stale coffee had worn off. Sam White Horse was trying to pull his gloves off so he could rub his eyes, when static from his radio broke through his fugue. "That you, boss?"

"Yeah Sam. What is your twenty?"

"Last patrol of the night. I wonder why it is so quiet out here. Think it might be the driving winds and the blowing snow?"

"OK Sam don't be a smart ass. Listen the power is back and I got a fax here you might be interested in. I know you want to go home, but I really think you might be interested in what I got. I'll put a fresh pot on."

"Why not. This was the last section I was going to check on anyway. See you in a few." Smacking his hat against the outside wall, stomping his boots on the mat outside the office. "OK Nathan, I'm here. What's up? I'm about to crash and burn right here."

Nathan Green, about sixty years old, portions of his long braids were gray streaked. His skin a weathered brown, Deep laugh lines, and a stomach that hid his belt bukle, standing and pouring coffee in a deep ceramic cup with the name Sam on the side. Handing the cup to Sam, and sitting behind an old splintered desk. "Well Sam it seems everyone in three states is looking for a blue cargo van. Got pictures of the van with Montana tags outside a bait shop. Inside the shop the clerk had his throat slit. It is also possible that a Melvin Wright the registered owner of the van has abducted a little girl."

"OK Nate, why did you call me back here? Shouldn't I be tracking him down?"

"Sam you told me he took off. No need to try and track in this weather. The little girl is still in the hospital. Right?"

"You got an address to go with that registration?"

"Yeah, but I think we need to try and get this little girl back with her parents."

"Well Nathan what do you want me to do."

"I'm calling Rides The Horse," Looking over at Sam. "To relieve you. You get back to the hospital make sure nobody tries to move that baby."

Sam went into the small locker room, threw cold water on his face, dug in his locker for a clean dry pair of socks, threw the damp socks on the bottom of the locker, and changed his shirt. Bundled up he headed back for the SUV. Calling back to Nathan, "OK Lieutenant, I'm heading back for the hospital."

By the time he got back to the parking lot his SUV had a thick layer of snow covering it. *I can't believe this. I was sure the storm had let up.* The flakes were thick. By the time he got to the SUV the wind was blowing and the snow was coming down sideways.

In the ICU, Sam pulled a folding chair outside the cubical that Jackie was in. A doctor and Running Deer were in and out of the small cubical. Sam thought he knew the doctors here and the few nurses that worked in the hospital. There seemed to be two doctors. The only reason he assumed they were doctors was stethoscopes around their necks. He recognized one of the doctors, but did not recall ever seeing the short dark one He had no idea how long it would take Robert Rides The Horse to relieve him; time doesn't hold that much meaning for his Crow brother. He walked to the reception area looking for the coffee pot. Karen was still sitting at her desk with her head over her computer. Looking up with a start, "Sam I told you about sneaking up on people."

"Sorry. Just waiting for Rides The Horse, to relieve me. Say, I don't think I've ever seen this many medicos here. This being a Public Health hospital and all plus the last I heard this place is not a real hospital."

"There were doctors in earlier. Something about letting us be a hospital again. There was a couple doctors in from Billings. Got stuck by the storm. One doctor attempted to get to a motel. One doctor stayed here to help out with our one and only patient.

Turning back toward Sam, "Must be the storm. I've working his shift for a while now, but for some reason I can barely keep my eyes open." Pouring coffee in her mug, then just staring at the coffee, "I swear Sam if I even have another sip of this coffee, I'll be up for the next eight hours just running back and forth to the bathroom; course I could just go to sleep on the pot."

Wiping her eyes with her knuckles, Karen stretched and walked back over to her desk, stopping in front of her desk, "Sam this may come as a surprise, but the coffee is fresh."

"That alone will keep me awake."

Pacing back and forth, then looking at Sam, "Sandra is supposed to be my relief. Katie Woods, the Admin Supervisor, said she'd be in first thing in the morning; don't really know what that means."

"Well, Karen we may both be waiting. It doesn't look like this storm is going to stop anytime soon."

Chapter 9

Naomi's phone rang at 4:30 in the morning. Naomi put her phone on speaker and woke Russell. It was Myra, Russell's mother, "Kids, I know you are going through a real black time. Have you heard anything about Jacquelyn?"

Russell picked up the phone, held it out so that Naomi could hear it, "They are telling us that they are sure Jackie is no longer in Louisiana."

"I really hate to tell you but Dad is in the hospital. He went in for his normal check-up and it was decided that he would need to stay. The doctor told me that they need to get him ready." Looking up at Naomi, his mother continued, "Sorry your dad has a problem with the way I think too. They are expecting his lung and heart will be here by Friday. You know it's funny, he wasn't acting any different. The cough wasn't even that bad. The only thing different was that he hadn't had a cigarette all day. It was as if he knew they would be calling today. Listen if you don't think you can make it, I'll understand."

Russell looked over at Naomi. She nodded her head. "Mom we will be leaving here shortly. We are not going anyplace but Texas until we know what's going on with dad."

The Gallagher's reluctantly checked out of the motel and at Agent Williams' suggestion bought a cellular phone. He gave the number to Agent Williams, and after feeding the boys and three cups of coffee for both Naomi and him they were once again on the road heading for Houston Texas.

Russel looking, looking, "Naomi, would you look for the turn off to Deer Park?" Shaking his hands one at a time, "Don't know why but staring at the side of the road looking for highway signs has me roaming all over the road. Good thing it's not rush hour."

"Russ I think we are supposed to be looking for the Center Street exit."

Surprisingly, at least for Russ he found himself in a driveway and his mother standing out on the front patio. "OK boys. You see that woman in front of that door?"

Denny piped up, "Oh dad I know grandma." Anthony chimed in, "Me too."

Before Russ had the car completely stopped, and Naomi could say another word, the boys were out of the car.

"Hey Myra, sorry things aren't going to well for either of us."

With tears in her eyes, "I just got back from the VA. Bryan says he feels about like he always does. You know a little tightness in his chest. Says there doesn't seem to be any new pains. But you people have to be going through your own kind of hell. You know me and dad have had our time, and I know that this time here of earth is only temporary." Looking at her son and grabbing Naomi's hand, "But this baby has a whole life to look forward to. I've been bending our Good Lord's ear daily. I'm at the day chapel at the church. Sometimes three or four times in a day. If I'm not here I'm at the chapel at the VA."

Naomi looking at Myra, "You know mom, I can't think of anyone else I'd rather have praying for me, and Jackie than you, don't get me wrong I'll accept everybody's prayers. Believe me our prayers with Bryan and you as well. You know we should be celebrating Russ made it home."

Asa was sitting at his desk across from Tom Walton. Even with the air-conditioner on and the ceiling fans turning he had his the knot on his tie pulled half way down his open blue long sleeve dress shirt with large sweat stains around the armpits, tropical weight suit jacket was hanging on the back of his chair. There was a time when he first started with the Bureau that the only color shirt that was recognized was white, and agents were considered out of uniform without heir suit jackets on. The red light on his desk phone started blinking, and then the old fashioned ring. It startled him as since the advent of the cellular phone the land lines were rarely heard especially in Baton Rouge. Picking up the phone receiver, "Special Agent Williams."

"Is that you Asa?"

"You got me friend."

"Friend is it? This is Nathan Green. Don't blame you for not recognizing me. What's it been thirty years since we shared a hooch in Nam?"

With a brief hesitation, and scratching his head, "More like forty years. Chief? Where the hell you calling from?"

"Its lieutenant, Crow Tribal Police. You know I never did like being called Chief."

"OK Nathan what have you got for me."

"I got your fax, and the picture of the little girl, and I'm pretty sure we have your little girl up here. I haven't seen her yet, but one of my patrolmen identifies the picture you sent to us. She's in pretty bad shape, but I'm sure it's her and she is in the hospital here in Agency Montana. My officer Sam White Horse was there when she was checked in."

"Has she been molested?"

"I haven't had a chance to look at her, but I don't think she has been molested. She is being treated for double pneumonia. The bastard that brought her in has vamoosed. We'll keep an eye on her. Seems like the state of Montana is snowed in right now, the closest airfield is in Billings, and it has been closed and probably will be for a while."

"Nathan, the Bureau has their own air force."

"Do your best Asa. Be sure to bring your foul weather gear."

"Nathan, that is amazing. Here in Baton Rouge we have the air-conditioner plus the ceiling fans running at full blast; well the fans may not be at full blast."

After waiting in line for fifteen minute he handed the keys to his car to a valet. Russ thought he was at the Veterans Administration Hospital, Myra pointed out that the sign above the door stated that they were entering The Michael E DeBakey VA Medical Center.

"Wow you guys are really gong downtown." Remarked Naomi.

Naomi, Myra, Russ with the two boys headed into the VA. "Mom, are we going to get any flak bringing the boys in with us? Asked Russell."

"No Russell, your boys are, or appear to be well behaved. I'm sure it will be OK." Russ stopped and looked down at his leg; he was feeling a vibration. Hearing music, other than what was coming over the VA speaker system. What?"

"Russell, that's your phone." Naomi remarked with a slight grin. Stepping off to the side putting the phone up to his ear, "Hello, Hello?" Naomi grabbed his phone, "Russ tap the phone here."

"Mr. Gallagher, now I don't want you to get your hopes up, but I think we have located Jackie."

"I'll be there."

"Sir I'm just keeping you up to date on what we are doing. Let me check this out first."

Naomi reached over Russell's shoulder and put the cell phone of speaker, "Special Agent Williams, this is Naomi. Where is my baby?"

"We think she may be in Montana. Tom and I will be flying up there as soon as the weather clears."

"Naomi again. Its 80 degrees outside. What's wrong with the weather?"

"I know, Louisiana is hot and humid, but Billings Montana is below zero with blowing snow. Let me do my job. I'll call you as soon as I have anything."

Bryan Gallagher had a breathing tube in his nose, he was hooked up to an IV. There was a kindle propped on his knees. Looking up, "Hey gang are these two guys my grandsons?"

Russell spoke. "Yeah pop. It's been a while, but if you remember the little one with the, what do I call it? The platinum hair is Anthony, and this other guy is Dennis."

"Russell I might be dying, but I am not feeble. It is true they have grown like weeds since the last time I saw them."

With his eyes starting to water, Russell remarked, "Are you really that anxious to leave us?"

"No son, I'm not, but I am not about to tell myself stories. Listen surgery is still a possibility. Fact is the reason I'm here now is for them to pump me up with antibiotics. They're expecting my new plumbing in by Friday. Now what is going on with that little girl of ours, Jacquelyn? Have you heard anything?"

"Yeah pop. The FBI agent called telling me that he thinks he knows where she is." Leaving the VA, and Bryan in pretty good spirits, and heading back to Deer Park.

Russell looks back at Naomi and then at is mother, "My God how do you people handle this traffic?"

Giving Russell a playful punch on his shoulder, "Well son I try to avoid it."

From the back seat Anthony is literally pounding on is father's shoulder, "Daddy, daddy, please listen to me?"

Glancing back over his shoulder Russell replies, "What is it Anthony?"

"Daddy, daddy, Jackie is in a plastic tent. She has a tube in her nose and there are bottles with rubes coming out of them into her arms. There is a big tube coming out of her chest"

With a breath Russ glances back at Naomi, Naomi are you hearing this. "Yes Russ I heard."

Just then Denny looks at his mom and reaches up to touch his father, "Please mom, dad, listen to Anthony?"

Naomi speaks up, "Boys we are all upset, but please this is nonsense. There is no way you could possibly know where your sister is."

Myra looking over at her son and then glancing back at Naomi, with a look of discomfort, "What is this all about?"

"Well mom," Naomi replies, "Anthony thinks he knows where Jackie is, and Denny doesn't help he also thinks that Anthony knows where she is. I really don't need this."

"Naomi, don't be too hard on your boys. You know they are also having dealing with losing their sister. Truthfully Naomi I cannot imagine what you are going through."

Leaning forward, "Myra, you are going through your own hell, and now this?"

"Don't get me wrong. Bryan and I have been married for almost fifty years. This ...what we are going through is all a part of life. Believe me he has been a real pain at times, but if something happens I still know I'll miss him."

Glancing to his right, "Mom, the sign says the next three exits. Which one do I take?"

"Take the one that says Center."

Sitting in his father's recliner, and kicking off his shoes, "Naomi, would you come over here for a minute?"

Sitting on the couch next to Russell, "OK. What's up?"

"Well that call that came in on my cell while we were entering the VA?"

"Yeah?"

"That was Special Agent Williams. He says that they got a tip from the Tribal Police up in Montana. They think Jackie might be in the Public Health Service Hospital."

Rising from the couch, and heading for the bedroom, "Well come on what are you waiting for. My baby is in some strange hospital. We have to be with her."

Walking into the room Myra Wiping her hands on a dish towel, "I hope you don't mind but your boys are out back with a few boys from the neighborhood."

"No mom. I hope they know enough to stay close."

"I did tell them and asked if they would please stay in our yard."

"Naomi and I were just talking about the phone call I got while we were at the hospital. Special Agent Williams, that's the FBI agent that is in charge of finding our baby. Anyway there has been a sighting of what they believe is Jacki. As soon as the weather clears he's going to check it out." looking over at his wife, "Naomi wants to go up to Montana that is where she was supposedly spotted. The agent asked that we stay here. He says he was just keeping us informed, and he would prefer us not come just yet, or at least until he is sure it is Jacki."

The house phone rang. The color in Myra's face was completely drained. Looking down at the caller ID, "Yes." Picking up the receiver and listening, "Yes. This is Mrs. Gallagher." Gently placing the receiver back on the cradle. "That was the VA. They had hoped schedule his surgery for the end of the week. Seems they just found a match. They are taking him in for surgery tonight."

Grabbing her purse Naomi looked up to see Anthony and Dennis standing by the car.

As Russell and Myra climbed into the car, "What is this?" looking at the boys, asked Naomi.

Anthony replied. "We are going back to the hospital?"

Russell grabbed Anthony's shoulder, "Were you listening while Grandma was on the phone?"

With raised eyebrows, "No. Just knew."

Chapter 10

Looking in the refrigerator, "Melvin somebody has been in our refrigerator."

"What?"

"I said somebody has been here since we were here a few hours ago."

With a bag half full Melvin came out to the kitchen. Opening the refrigerator, and looking in. "There's no food in here, but that ain't unusual. How do you know that somebody's been here?"

"Well… there was pickles in the door, the jar is in the trash can. Any other food that was in there was starting to grow weird stuff on it, plus it stank, so I threw other stuff out when we were here before. I know I didn't throw out the pickles. They actually taste better when they been in there a while."

"Darlene that is discussing."

"It's just a little spooky."

"That's why we got to get out of here. Now get what you think you're going to need, and let's get out of here before they come back or the weather gets worse."

Climbing in the van, Melvin hears music, "I think your purse is playing music." Digging in the bag she calls a purse, Darlene pulled out her cell phone. "I don't understand I didn't pay the bill, but the phone seems to be working just fine."

Throwing the bags into the van, Melvin points to the van, "Darlene, get in and buckle up. I'm just gona check our crib out. You know make sure all the lights are out, make sure we haven't forgotten anything."

Music again. Melvin stopped and turned back towards the van. "Is that the phone again?"

Digging it out of her bag once more, "Hello? This is Darlene. He's right here."

"What's up? That you Larry?"

"Yes my friend this is Al-Abadi Labeeb. I am at the Public Health Hospital."

"How did you know your package was there?"

"Listen Melvin, it was not that hard to figure it out. Were you just going to leave her here?"

"A Tribal policeman was getting a little too curious."

"So you taking off will stop him from checking on you?"

"Probably not, but if I take off now he may not be able to find me."

"Well my friend, find a good place to hide. I will take care of our package." Climbing back out of the van, "I'm just going back in to make sure nothing is out of place."

A few minutes later Melvin is back in the truck. "Darlene, did you leave the lid off the peanut butter? You also left a spoon in the jar."

"Melvin I did not even look in the cupboard. I forgot we had peanut butter."

With his eyebrows raised, turning to look at Darlene, "OK. That's enough of that. Let's just get out of here."

"It must have been Larry."

Pulling out of his snow crusted driveway, "I think I know a place we can stay off the radar. There is a little town I know that is up in the mountains of Colorado. If anybody even thinks about us..." Darlene was just staring at him. Well they'll soon forget. They normally only search for kids and people like us for a few days. They just don't have the money or manpower to keep looking."

Looking over at Melvin, "What's the deal with this Larry guy?"

"We really need to get off the Rez. Well I heard about this guy when I was at Angola. Larry gets online orders from all over the world. Very rich Arab, or Sultan; whatever they call them decides he needs to add another woman to his harem, or maybe they need somebody to do the cleaning, or wash their dishes. He sends people like me, you and me to fill orders. In the meantime, he and his friends got to have their fun and when they are done, the product may be slightly used, will be shipped out to their destinations, some as far away as Bosnia and Thailand. Some may stay here in the states. There are a lot of rich whites, both men and women they like having help around the house. Then there are the women that don't want to have a baby. It might just mess up their figure. Oh, they want a new born. This is the first time to my knowledge that he has requested one of this age. I guess if they get them at four or five they don't have to house train them.

Feeling the van slide, Melvin tightened his grip on the steering wheel. "Ya know I've done business with Larry before. He normally wants girls and women from Indian reservations. You know teenage girls that aren't far from working the streets. Especially one that have been kicked out of their homes. He always pays well, and the girls I pick up don't normally give me much hassle; they're hungry and cold and ready to get off the streets."

"But Melvin why that little one? Why did we have to go to Louisiana? You told me when we met you never, never wanted to go back to Louisiana?"

"I wasn't sure I was gona do this for him. But when we ran out of money... Anyway he had been tracking this little one for a while. He gave me the numbers on the Florida tags. I mean how hard could it be?"

Melvin turned off the main highway onto a farm to market road heading in the right direction that was not covered in snow and ice, or at least any ice he could see. The van was still skidding on the black ice he could not see."

Anthony was still in the trailer hiding in a closet in a room that didn't look like it was used much. He went back into the kitchen, found a spoon in a drawer, open the jar of peanut butter and took another spoonful. He had been to the hospital and gave Jacki her stuffed rabbit. He had to get back to the hospital. He felt something was wrong. Those bad people were not going back to the hospital. He had to get back to his sister.

He knew his sister was in a plastic tent in a hospital. He saw her. He put her bunny in the tent with her. What he didn't know was the name of the hospital. *Public Health? I guess that is as good a name as any. It's cold. This ain't Texas, or Florida.*

There was a different lady at the desk. She looked up and saw him, "Hello, I'm Mrs. Woods. Are you here with your folks?"

"Yeah...Yes mam. They went back to visit my sister."

"Who is you sister?"

What am I going to do now? Putting his hands up to his eyes, trying to snuffle and whimper like he was going to start to cry, "They don't want me in there cause they say I might make him sicker."

It worked she went back the desk and picked up some kind of magazine

Managing to slide past a very big policeman with long black hair he managed to get near Jackie's plastic tent. *There is a little dark man standing with other people in doctor clothes: long white doctor coats.* Anthony couldn't see his face; it was covered with a white mask, like what doctors wear. He did notice the little man's eyes. Anthony just knew he didn't look like the rest of the doctors. *Now I remember that is the man that was watching us at the airport.*

Mrs. Woods reminded Anthony of his grandma, but this lady was tan with brown eyes and a lot heavier than the other lady. The lady he was looking at had dark brown hair. *Grandma is white, most of the time, unless she has her cheeks painted red, plus her hair is mostly silver, and curly.*

Trying to get a closer look at his sister, one of the doctors, a tall skinny one looked directly at him, "What are you doing back here, son?"

"Sir that is my sister. How's she doing?"

"Where are your folks?"

"My mom needed to go home to get her medicine."

"Well, son you need to go wait out front. Let me know when your folks get back." Anthony didn't see Jackie's bunny. *I wonder if they throwed her bunny away.*

Robert Rides The Horse was sitting in a metal folding chair next to the desk occupied my Katie Wood. "Katie I'm going to grab a cup that coffee, and head back towards that baby. You got the duty today?"

"Actually Sandra was supposed to be here. Guess she's having trouble getting through the snow. I told Karen that she could crash here. I told her it was really hard to get through the blowing snow. She said she didn't live that far. She's supposed to call me when she gets home. I don't know what the bosses will say. You know we are not supposed to admit patients. What are you doing here?"

"Seems like there is a young one, I mean really young back there. Boss thinks she is a kidnap victim. I'm just going to grab this coffee and head back there. I relieved Sam a few minutes ago. Didn't take him much time to clear out of here."

Robert Ride The Horse was back at the coffee pot. There were a few people in the reception area, but nothing like most days, like when the winds were close to calm and the snow wasn't a foot deep. "Katie?"

Sliding her desk chair back and turning towards Robert, a little abrupt. "What is it Robert?"

"I'm sorry. Did I do something to upset you?"

"No Robert. It's just days like today seem to bring the worse out of me. Plus I was supposed to be working on our accounts. You know trying to figure out how we can take care of these people. Trying to figure out how we can get recertified so we can actually treat patients. I did hear from Sandra. Seems she is having a little trouble getting a baby sitter. Normally her kids would be in school; no school today."

Just then Robert's radio squelched. "Robert?"...static..."Robert, can you hear me?"

"You're weak."

"If the land line is....?"Screech...static... "Call dispatch."

"Will do."

"Say again. Did you copy?"

Picking up the receiver on the desk next to Katie, "Yes dispatch. Got a message to call you."

"Stand-by the Captain is getting on the line."

Scratching his head, Robert answers the Captain, "What can I do for you Cap?"

"How is the little girl doing?"

"I was just in there. She seems to be sleeping, although she has tubs coming out of her little body, and there are more doctors here than I have ever seen. Didn't know we had that many doctors. I thought they stayed in the big city where they actually got paid."

"Robert don't let anybody take her anyplace. She is apparently a kidnapping victim. As soon as they can fly into Billings the Feds will be here."

"Captain, I'm sitting right outside the little cubical. The lone bed was positioned near the opening in the curtains surrounding the cubical surrounded by IV racks, medical sensors, and several pieces of equipment. There were hoses, cables, and clear plastic tubing.

Hanging up the phone, "Katie, I guess it's just the two of us?"

"Not for long. While you were on that line, I got a call from Sandra. Seems they sent her husband home from work, so he is going to watch the kids." Looking up over half lens reading glasses, "It's not that you're not good company, but you need to be in there and I need to get a lot of paperwork done. This is the perfect day. Unless we get a ten car pile-up, I don't see very much business."

Sam made it through the weekend. He had been spending twelve hours at the hospital. It was 8:02 Am when Robert showed up to relieve Sam, "Give me a few minutes Sam. I need to use the head."

"Robert I know the Crow have a reputation of not letting time get in our way, but brother this staying in one spot is about to drive me up the walls. I've been pacing since four this morning, and if I even smell another cup of coffee, well you know the rest of it."

Robert was still pulling his trousers up as he came out of the restroom. "I am sorry Sam. Listen I'll be early tonight. I promise."

"Say… Robert I stepped outside a few minutes ago, and guess what I could see the mountains, and there was a strange light in the sky. Karen told me they call that the sun."

"OK, Sam. Just let me get something to eat and a few hours' sleep. Oh yeah, the Feds should be here tomorrow."

Sam sitting in the hard metal folding chair, stretching his long legs, finally getting up off the chair and pacing. Looking in on Jackie, and noticing that the tube in her chest had been removed. She still had a tube in each nostril, and an IV needle in her foot. There was that strange doctor left in the little cubical; a short dark man with what appeared to be dark stubble. He recognized the other doctor but there was something about this one.

Taking a deep breath in the frosty evening, looking up at a full moon; the first time he'd seen the moon in days. Thinking about sitting in his warm trailer with a cold beer; there had to be something on the tube. Just then he saw the dark little doctor. He had to ask, "Doctor, Doctor."

The little man whose face appeared to have a three day growth of dark whiskers, stopped and turned towards Sam, "Where you talking to me?"

"Yes. I haven't seen you around here before."

"Oh I'm Doctor Abadi. I'm a pulmonary specialist from Helena. I was down here to evaluate this Public Health hospital. I got stranded by the blizzard. That little girl in there was in pretty bad shape. So I offered my assistance." Heading back towards Jackie, "I understand that this is not a real hospital."

Calling after the doctor, "This was a hospital up to a few months ago. The only hospital available for the people here and as far south as Lodge Grass."

The waiting room was starting to fill up. Looked like everyone waited for the snow to stop and the roads to be plowed. Sam took one more deep breath, and squinted against the red sun setting behind a snow white mountain that appeared to be reaching for a rapidly changing sky from an azure to indigo.

Coming back inside, rubbing his hands together, making a fist and blowing into each hand. Most everyone had left. There was one nurse in with the child, a doctor in the ER, and a nurse practitioner. Nurse Running Deer, one of the two nurses on staff that was covering the night shift. Standing directly in front of Sam as he came in the door, "I see you're here looking out for our little girl."

Taking off his coat and putting it on the back of the metal folding chair, "Yeah. You know don't you that everybody has to be someplace. By the way what do you know about that," pointing to the little man that looked like he needed a shave, "Doctor over there?"

"I've never seen him before. I guess he is here from medical board. It is curious. You know once the storm let up the other visitors were out of here so fast all I saw was a flash. Does he bother you Sam." Turning to the cubical, "You know nobody may any comments about the little girl. Even that doctor from Helena didn't make any comments about treating someone here."

"It's probably just my paranoia, but there's something about him that bothers me. How about you? You the only nurse on tonight?"

"No we'll have another nurse. The x-ray tech checked in." Running Deer was the head nurse and it seemed to Sam that she was fully in charge. One of the problems this little medical facility had was the lack of nurses. Most registered nurses went into Billings where the pay was slightly better.

Another doctor arrived. The waiting room was emptying rapidly. They were mainly dealing with minor injuries, a couple of belly aches. Walking outside and seeing a full moon, it did not surprise Sam when women in labor started coming in. It didn't surprise Running Deer either; she anticipated this and had scheduled the appropriate nurses.

Sam still squirming in the hard uncomfortable chair. He did notice the full moon, and was not surprised to see women obviously in labor coming in. Standing and stretching his long legs he became aware that the last time he had seen Dr. Abadi, he was leaning over Jackie. He looked in the cubical and the child seemed to be sleeping; only the IV line was left. He looked for the doctor. The little dark doctor was nowhere to be seen. Thinking to himself, *he probably finally took a break. Might have even gone back to his hotel, motel or wherever?*

Not that the passing of time was ever of great concern to Sam, but this night he was anxious for his relief. Robert did come in early; if a person were to call and say they were going to be late Sam rarely if ever experienced resentment or envy, but looking at a well-rested, clean faced Robert, made him think of an earlier time when he felt he didn't need rest or sleep. Standing up as Robert entered, "Good Morning Sunka Wakan."

"Sam, do I really look Lakota?"

"You know what the whites say? We all look alike."

"Anyway I had a very good night."

"Ah...you had a date. Not to worry the Feds should be here today, and our little girl seems to be recovering."

Chapter 11

An agent from the Helena field office was waiting for Agent Asa Williams Looking up with his hand out was a tall lanky blond haired man wearing a charcoal top coat and a fur cap, "You must be Special Agent Asa Williams," looking over at Tom, "and this must be The Agent Tom Walton I keep hearing about. I'm Agent Al Reed, out of the Helena field office. I would have thought you would be using the Bureau's Gulf Stream?"

"I guess neither one of us are high enough on the list for that; although they said when I'm ready to go home, they would send one. I really think the weather scared off the pilot. Pulling out a handkerchief and wiping his nose, "What was that?"

"Our car is outside. Do you guys have any other luggage?"

"No. Just my carry-on."

Stepping outside the terminal, Asa remarked, "I can see why you're wearing a top coat. How far to Crow Agency?"

"Not far, bout fifty miles. The roads have finally been plowed. Do you need a cup of coffee or maybe something to eat?"

"No I'm fine. I would just like to see that little girl."

Sitting in the right seat with Tom in the back seat, of the sedan, Asa scratched at his chin, "Man I have one dozy of a head ache," putting his head back on the head rest, and rubbing his throbbing temples, "and before you say anything. It is not a hangover."

Asa couldn't help but notice the mountain. Looking out at the pale blue sky. "You know Reed, I know now why that call this Big Sky country. It is truly amazing."

"Yes it is sir. I didn't think I'd like this assignment, but now if I were to get another assignment I don't think my wife and kids will come with me. By the way we are being followed."

89

Reaching up and turning the rearview mirror, "Your right. Is that a maroon Chevy? Tom, Tom take a look behind us."

Trying to re-adjust the rearview mirror, "Do you know this guy?"

First, stop calling me sir. It makes me feel old; I mean older. Damn, I'm pretty sure that is our victim's father. By the way, just don't call me sir when we are out of the office."

"Yes sir. I mean yes."

Scrubbing a hand over his face, Asa asked, "Reed, find a place to pull over. I told these people to wait until I could confirm that we did in fact have their daughter."

Tom Walton leaned up against the front seat. Tapping Al Reed on the shoulder, "Is there going to be other agents at the hospital?"

Pulling on the shoulder of the road, and turning to look at Reed, "The Helena office is not that big, but there will be a few more agents there. You know we have to be nice, nice to the tribal police. There were very helpful and the police superintendent said he would be able to spare a few of his patrolmen."

Tom Commented, sarcastically, "That was mighty considerate of him."

Agent Al Reed turned to Tom, "We have a very good relationship with the tribal police. It is true it has taken a while to gain their trust. When they heard that the little girl that they have in the Public Health Service hospital might be a kidnap victim, the tribal police were more than willing to help."

The agents had stopped on the shoulder, and within a minute the Chevy pulled in behind them. Asa climbed out of the sedan. Breathing deeply Asa tapped on the window of the Chevy, after the window was rolled down, "Mr. Gallagher just what are you doing?"

Looking up at Asa, "That is my child and we have a right to be here."

Abruptly, at first. Then with another breath and letting it out slowly, and deliberately calming and softening his voice, "Mr. Gallagher...Russell. We don't know what we will be dealing with. If the person, or people that took you child is here this whole situation may get out of hand. I am concerned about Jackie's safety, and now I have to be concerned about your safety. I have to say this, you being here might very well cost us by either allowing the suspects to get away or endangering your daughter. And by the way did you have to bring your entire family. Whatever happens you people are going to make this whole procedure much, much harder."

"I'm sorry, and we will stay out of your way. But if that is Jackie in that hospital, she is going to want to be with her mother."

"Russell, you're right, but I cannot have you anywhere near that hospital. If your child is in there I will call you as soon as I know it is safe. Just stay close."

Agent Reed turned to Asa, "There is a café not far outside Crow Agency. Why don't the Gallagher's stop in at the little café and wait for us? They'll be close enough that it will only take minutes for them to get to the hospital."

Asa looked over at Al Reed, and then at Russell, "What do you think?"

Russell considering, then staring back at his car and Naomi, "That sounds like a good idea."

Walking back to the government sedan, "Where is this café you're talking about?" inquired Asa.

"It's not far from the hospital. It just a little further on I-90."

"Russell. You people follow us. We'll signal to you at the café."

No more than ten minutes passed when the government car signal for Russ and his family to turn into the café parking."

The parking lot was fairly crowded for early afternoon. Russell was looking for a spot close enough yet also in a place where if needed he could get on the highway. There was a rusted our blue van at the edge of the parking lot not far from the highway. Out of the back seat. "Daddy, Mommy! Over there." Screamed Anthony.

Naomi turned to look back at Anthony, "What Anthony? What are you screaming about?"

"Look. Near the highway."

Just then there was an amplified sound like fingernails scraping across a chalkboard? "Russell! Pull over near that van."

"Naomi. Use you cell phone and call Agent Williams."

"Already done he's on his way back here. The car is on the way back. He'll just get out here and his partner will go on to the hospital."

For Russ and Naomi, waiting for Agent Williams seemed to be taking forever. Every time Russ was looking at his watch every minute. One minute seemed like an hour.

Denny from the back seat literally punched his father's shoulder, "Dad look," pointing to the van, "They're getting away."

With that Naomi pushed the door open and jumped out, running towards the van and then seeing the woman with the mousy brown hair, she screamed, "Oh no you don't." coming up on the woman the smell of the woman just about took her breath. Thinking, *I'll never forget that putrid smell.*

Russell falling out of the car, "Naomi no! Come back here." The man yelled, "Darlene, look out!"

By then Naomi had a handful of that mousy brown hair, "No you don't. You are going to give me back my baby."

"Aaaa! Get off me. Melvin help me."

Melvin started to grab Naomi as Russell came up and put his arm around the much bigger man's neck. Melvin tried to turn, but found this much smaller wiry man hard to get away from. Russell squeezing tighter and tighter on the man's throat with his forearm. Melvin tried to turn into Russell's elbow, but was finding the hold that Russell had on him impossible to break lose. Melvin saw gray and then black. Russ felt Melvin go limp and letting go, watched as Melvin collapsed to the ground. Naomi made a fist and putting her whole body into her punch. She felt bone, and mush as she looked to see Darlene's smashed, and bloodied nose. With her hand up to her nose, Darlene fell unconscious to the ground. Naomi was about to jump on top of her. She could see herself killing this woman; the one that smelled like bad fish. There was no mistaking that this is the woman that knocked **her,** Naomi, out and took her baby.

"Anthony do you hear that?" asked Denny.

"Sounds like a serene of a police car. I guess the blue and red lights are from the police too." Commented Anthony.

The government car with Agent Williams stopped and Asa jumped as the car sped off. Rubbing his knees and thinking, *I really do have to retire; that hurt.* Running or a close facsimile of a run and Agent Williams got up to the state patrol car, out of breath and reaching for his Identification, as the trooper reached for his side arm. Gasping for breath he managed to get out, "Wait. FBI.

While the trooper took the FBI credentials out of Asa's hand, Melvin grabbed Darlene by her hair managed to wake her and they both stagger to the van, with dirt, gravel and a cloud of dust they fishtailed onto the still slick highway.

Bending over and trying to catch his breath; just trying to breathe. Williams stood up, reached out with a shaky hand and grabbed his ID back and looking as the van disappear down the highway, "Shit!"

With a very dumb expression the trooper looked at Asa, "Is there a problem Agent?" Staring directly into the troopers eyes, "No trooper no problem other than you allowing our suspects to get away."

"When I rolled up they appeared to be the victims, and that," Pointing to Naomi, "would have killed her if I didn't restrain her."

"Would that have been so bad?"

"I was sworn to enforce the law, and the two of them, both him and the woman were about to kill someone."

"Trooper let me ask you a question?"

The trooper just gave Williams a defiant look.

"Trooper...Before you go out on patrol, or at the start of your shift. Don't answer, just listen. Do you guys get together for a briefing; you know a little meeting. To see if there just might be something to look for while cruising these highways. Well if you had you would have seen or been told of a pair of murderers and kidnappers we have wants and warrants on. Oh if you didn't notice every police agency has pictures of the couple we are looking for and that blue van. It is believed that the man you just released has killed at least one police officer, and probably more than a few civilians. Williams was evidently still out of breath. He just motioned to the trooper as if he were shooing a fly away. The trooper wasted no time in getting in his cruiser and departing. Agent Asa Williams barely staggered towards the Gallagher's car. Naomi stepped out of the car and left the door open. Grabbing onto the roof of the Caprice, Asa almost fell, but did manage to plop on the seat.

Naomi noticed that Asa complexion went from almost purple to a very pale white. Motioning for Russ to come and help her. "Agent Williams are you alright?"

Taking a breath and holding his chest, and reaching in his breast pocket, "I don't suppose you got any aspirin in this car?"

Denny spoke up, "Mom, there is aspirin in the first aid kit. It's in the glove box." Handing Asa the aspirin, and a bottle of water, Naomi asked, "should I call an ambulance?'

"Thanks. I'm tempted, but I do feel better and we have to get your baby." Russ looked at the agent, "Listen. Don't you dare drop dead on us?"

Finally able to take a deep breath and letting it out slowly, Asa looked up at Naomi and then at Russ and the boys, "Thank you. This has happened before. I normally have Nitroglycerin in my pocket. The Nitro must have fallen out of my pocket when I was running. I would appreciate it if you didn't mention this to my partner. I've got less than a year to go for retirement. Plus as soon as I get back to Louisiana I make a point to seeing my doctor."

Chapter 12

Pulling into the parking lot of the Public Health Service Hospital, Sam couldn't help looking towards the mountain range and the setting sun. It looked to him as if once again business was as usual. Walking into the emergency room, there was the familiar odor of alcohol, antiseptic an assortment of body fluids, and the all too recognizable smell of blood with the underlying stench of old pennies. The orderlies and the staff did an excellent job of keeping the area clean, but Sam had always had an acute sense of smell.

Robert was seated at the admittance cubical talking with Sandra. Walking over to Robert interrupting what appeared to be a very animated conversation, "How's our little girl today?"

"The last time I looked she was sleeping. Looks like all the tubes and monitors have been removed. She woke up a while ago crying wanting her momma, but the doctor gave her a sedative, and she has been sleeping ever since."

"I thought we agreed to stay in that chair, by her cubical? Well let's go back and check on her?"

Turning to go back to where the child had been sleeping, Running Deer was coming out. "Evning Sam."

"Running Deer. How's our little girl doing?"

"Just came on shift. I'm heading back that way now."

They were at the cubical in less than a minute. Looking over at the day nurse, "How's our little girl doing?"

The nurse looking a bit bewildered, raising an eyebrow, "There are no children in here. I did notice a child when I came on, but since we are not supposed to except patients I assumed she was to be transported to Billings."

Running Deer feeling a catch in her chest, putting her hand on her breast, "Who authorize her move?"

"There was a short Mideast looking doctor standing by her bed." Running Deer was getting tense, the color in her face became chalky. "Do you have any paperwork on a Jackie Prescott?"

The nurse went to the nurse's station and looked through the paperwork. It seemed like it was taking a long time. She went through the paper work twice, "Nothing."

Sam and Running Deer were now running to the cubical where she was last seen. Sam looked where he saw her last. There was an old man lying on the thin examining bed, the one that had been Jackie's. Turning to the nurse. "There has to be paperwork on this child."

"No sir the last thing I saw was one of the visiting doctors hovering over her bed. When I came back I was informed that the bedding needed to be changed."

Running Deer spoke up, and as calmly as she could, she asked, "OK. How long has it been?"

The nurse was now beginning to sweat, even though between the cold outside and the air-conditioning the clinic felt like a meat locker. Looking over at Running Deer, "I suppose it's too late to call a code yellow?"

Agents Reed and Walton had just arrived at reception, Walton spoke to the receptionist. "We're here to see a patient. A little three-year-old, Jackie."

The receptionist raising her head, then looking down at what appeared to be some kind of roster, "What's the child's last name?"

Tom Walton looked at the receptionist, "I don't know, but you can't possibly have that many three-year-olds in the ICU."

"Well sir, first we do not have an ICU. I don't see any anyone on our roster. We are not supposed to be accepting patients."

At that moment there was a loud screech, followed by static, then the PHS's speaker system sounded an alarm, then the announcement that a code yellow, code yellow was in progress.

Agent Reed walked over to the receptionist, and calmly asked, "What is a code yellow?"

"Oh one of our patients, not that we have inpatients, has probably wondered off. It happens a lot with some of our older patients."

The people at Crow Agency were used to seeing a tribal police cruiser, but rarely saw a cruiser with the sheriff's marking on it and the State Police markings on the cruisers that were parked near the entrance to the clinic were even less likely to be seen.

Karen had just sat down at her desk, what she heard sounded like a heard of wild horses. She looked up to see men in police uniforms and two men wearing suits, one had on a tan top coat, the other man had a blue top coat draped over his arm more. Both top coats looked more like heavily lined trench coats. Out of habit she looked down at their shoes. Thinking, *nobody in these parts wear shoes like that. There is absolutely no way to keep a high gloss shine on shoes in this part of "Big Sky Country."*

Standing over the receptionist desk and looking down at Karen, "Where is the Gallagher child?"

Pushing her chair back away from the desk, "Agents, I just arrived here, but it seems that the child, that I had been calling Jackie Prescott has been transferred to the hospital at Billings."

Agent Tom Walton moved Agent Al Reed out of the way and stepped forward, "Who authorized the transfer?"

"Sir, I can't find any paperwork on the child."

"There was supposed to be a police officer next to the child. Where was the police officer?"

"Like I said, I just came on shift. I don't know, but I'm sure that if he was supposed to be stationed next to the child, he was. There must have been a doctor or other person in charge that authorized the transfer. I'm sure it was a medical emergency."

"Don't parents or guardians have to be not only notified but give permission?"

"When the woman claiming to be her guardian ran out of here, she became a ward of the state. Oh, we made several attempts to contact her, but nothing."

"Surely you have paperwork authorizing Child Protective Services guardianship of a sick child?" Asked Agent Walton.

Karen, had just taken off her lamb skin Jacket and was about to put it back on, as she was feeling cold. Looking up at the FBI agents she started to sweat, and no longer felt the need for her jacket. Going through the paperwork on her disordered desk, then rifling through the filing cabinet

She found what she was looking for. "Agents it appears Child Protective Services never really came here."

Tom spoke up, "What do you mean they never came?"

"The blizzard was once again howling, and there was no way a social worker could get here." Raising her hand to quiet the FBI agents, "I do have verbal authorization, with a file number. There was supposed to be someone here today to check in on the child."

Al Reed spoke up, "Did Child Protective Services Take the child?"

Karen's eyes were starting to water, "No sir. I have no paperwork indicating that she was removed by Child Protective Services. I will phone them right now."

Agent Asa Williams and the Gallagher's walked through the doors. Agent Williams went over to his partner, Naomi just stood still staring at the commotion in front of her. Anthony was yelling something, his brother Denny's eyes were red and tears were flowing. Russell was trying to console both boys. Holding his boys close and reaching for his wife, "What is happening here?"

Asa Williams motioned for the Gallagher's to come closer, "I am so sorry."

Naomi had no more tears to shed. Her voice was weak and raspy, "Why are you sorry agent? Is my child alive?"

"Yes she is alive, and her health is much better." Gazing outside the door and then looking at the Gallagher's, "The people here think she may have been taken to a hospital in Billings. We have someone checking with the hospitals in Billings right now."

The reception area of PHS was starting to thin out, most all law enforcement had departed. There were a few people waiting to be seen. There was only one doctor and he specialized in emergency medicine, the nurses available were pediatric nurses and spent most of their time with the women in labor. Nurse Running Deer was doing the best she could in assisting the doctor.

Standing over the reception desk, Agent Tom Walton asked, "Karen. Your name is Karen?" He got her attention, "So this is not a hospital?"

"It used to be, but because of funding, and the lack of qualified personnel we are not supposed to operate as a hospital. The doctors, right now there are three doctors, are well qualified, and with one exception the registered nurses are more familiar with pediatrics, and maternity."

Scratching his head, "So what is your function here?"

"My function is to act as a receptionist. We can still act as a clinic, but most of our patients are here to have babies. We do care for the occasional emergency."

"One more thing. How did our little girl, Jackie Gallagher wind up here?" asked Agent Walton.

"A man and a woman came in here. They said they were from Lodge Grass. There clinic turns into a first aid station and fire department at night. The man and woman claimed to be the little girl's guardians."

Denny noticed the policeman with his hair in braids standing near the entry to the little clinic. Turning to his brother, "Anthony, do you see that Indian standing," pointing to a tall brown skinned man the far side of the room. "Over there."

"I see him."

"Well is he a policeman or an Indian?"

"Denny, we are on an Indian reservation, and yes he is a policeman and an Indian.

"Russell, Naomi, from what I could find out your daughter is recovering from pneumonia.

She is no longer critical. We have checked with all the hospitals in the area. We will check all the hospitals in the state, and beyond. What I would really like you to do is go home, take care of the rest of your family. I promise that as soon as we find out anything I will be in contact with you. Let me know where you will be. I know you had been staying in Houston. When you go back to St. Pete call me."

Walking out with the Gallagher's to their car, Asa Williams bent down to the open passenger window, "I promise I will not stop until we find your baby."

Naomi looked up at Agent Williams, "Why here? What reason would they have to bring my baby here?"

"Naomi I really don't know how to answer that. I guess it might have been random, but my friend Nathan, he is a lieutenant on the tribal police, tells me that there has been several Indian women missing. The bureau has been investigating with the tribal police the tribal police for missing young girls and women. Mostly teen agers looking for a way out of poverty.

In general, accurate statistics on human trafficking victims are difficult to nail down because many women who manage to return are shamed into not reporting it. But I can tell you that in Northeastern Montana, we have definitely seen an increase in Native women who have been trafficked—an increase of 12 to 15 percent in the last year. They normally range in age is from 15 years old into their early 20s. I've seen reports that some of the women were as old as 50. Taking babies is brand new." Turning away from the car, "Just one other thing. I don't think whoever did this was planning on keeping her here in Montana."

Walking away from the Gallagher's, Asa turned, "I am sorry that was very unprofessional of me. I know that did nothing to help you. I think it was probably for my benefit to hear myself say it. We will get Jackie back.

Chapter 13

The trip back to Houston was uneventful, and very quiet. The boys barely spoke. Russell was driving and hand his head on Naomi's knee. "Naomi, I'm at a loss. I don't know what to do next." Commented Russell.

"Russ, when we left Houston your dad was about go home. He is your father and we really need to check in on him. I've spoken to Myra, she says he seems to be recovering well. That he was told to exercise, but not to overdo it."

"You know my dad doesn't know how to not overdo it. When he drinks he has to drink more than anyone else. And you know how he smoked. Some people might say my dad has an addictive personality." Putting both hands on the steering wheel, pulling down the car's sun visor, and squinting into the sun. "But you are right we do need to check in with the folks before we head back to Tampa Bay."

Naomi reached up next to her visor and removed sunglasses hand handed them to Russ, while she put her sun glasses on. "Do we go home and back to work, continue with our lives like nothing has changed?"

"Of course not. We try to focus on living our lives. I will never give up looking for our daughter. Going back to work and trying to focus will be the hardest thing I will ever do."

Naomi turning to look back at the boys, "You guys are awful quiet back there. What's going on?"

Denny leaned up against the front seat, "I know I used to complain about my baby sister, but you know I miss her, and I don't know if I'll ever be able to act as if everything is normal."

Denny and his mother both looked over at Anthony. Antony was just staring out the window. Naomi called, Anthony," Louder,

"Anthony!" looking directly at Denny, "Denny, shake your brother." Still nothing. No movement, nothing. "Is he breathing?"

"Yes mom he is breathing," putting his hand on his brother's cheek, and trying to turn Anthony's head. With some difficulty he managed to slightly turn his brother's head, "but his eyes are open. It's like he is in a deep sleep."

Russ glancing over at his wife, "What's going on?"

"I don't know what is going on with your son,"

"Something wrong with Denny?"

"No, your other son; you know the white one." Replied Naomi.

"Naomi that is not even funny."

"Denny is he hot, or cold?"

"No mom. He's just sleeping sitting up with his eyes open."

"Have you ever seen him do this before?"

"Yes Mam. The other night in the motel room I got up to go to the bafroom, and he just sat straight up with his eyes open. I tried to talk to him, but he didn't answer."

"Denny, sweetie, just keep an eye on your brother, and let me know if he starts breathing funny, or anything else that might be different."

"OK. You do know my brother is just a little weird."

Letting out a breath, "I don't really want to hear that. Although I do sometimes wonder about your brother."

It was warm and muggy. Anthony found himself standing in front of a white cinderblock two-story building. Looking around he saw what looked to him like a construction site. There were cement slabs with pipes sticking out of them on the ground. He was looking at skeletons of houses in different stages soon to be homes. Except for the building he was in front of. It was a white cinderblock building near a very large lake. There weren't many windows where he was standing. Walking around the building he found a window on the lake side of the building. It was too high for him to see through. There were several plastic milk bottle containers. Stacking two of the milk bottle containers he managed to look through a very dirty window. The next thing he knew he was standing in the middle of a large empty room. In the middle of the room was a big gas oven.

There were double doors on the side of the room farthest from him. Opening up one of the doors and peeking in, he could see a nurse behind a counter. There were couches and chairs in the room with the nurse, and women, all shapes, sizes, and colors of women.

He just knew his sister had to be here. He went back the way he came in. next to where he entered was a stairwell. He carefully climbed the stairs. There were several darkened offices down a long gloomy hallway. He heard what sounded like children, he also heard babies crying. He carefully pulled a door open. What he saw were beds. There were small children in the beds. About a dozen beds; six on either side. There were sinks between each bed. There was a desk at the far end of beds in front of what looked to Anthony like a medicine cabinet. He expected to see a nurse, but there were no nurses that he could see.

She was just lying on a lumpy mattress with dirty yellowed sheets. Her eyes were open and he was sure she spotted him. She had her thumb in her mouth two of her fingers up her nose. She could move her arms and hands, but the rest of her body was tied to the dirty bed. She tried to get up but the straps kept her on the bed. The clothes she had on looked dirty and wet. The clothing that the others were wearing was also dirty.

Anthony's eyes popped open, turning to Denny, "What are you doing Denny?"

"Anthony you was sleepen with your eyes open. Scared mom, but I seen you do that before."

"Listen Denny, Jackie is in a big building or maybe a horspital with a bunch of other kids. I think they are gona a do sompum bad we got to get somebody to listen."

"Anthony I told them you knew, but they ain't gona listen to me either."

Russell tapped Naomi on the arm. "I'm getting tired. You want to stop for the night?"

"No let's find a place to eat. I'll take over the driving. How far are we from Houston?"

"I figure we got maybe another five hours."

Cokes, coffee and sandwiches and they were back on the road. It was sunset, the sun was behind them, and the winds had died to a light breeze. It was no longer cold, just a slight chill in the humid air. They still had several hour on the road but the humidity, and the smells of vegetation was a sign that they were getting closer to the gulf.

Naomi was driving when they pulled up into the senior Gallagher's driveway. According to the radio it was 80 degrees in Deer Park Texas. Myra and Bryan were both sitting in their wooden rocking chairs on the small porch. Popping the trunk, grabbing the luggage, while the boys ran up to their grandparents on the porch. In unison the boys yelled "Grandma, Grandpa we are here."

Denny was the first to ask, "Grandpa, what does it feel to have someone else's lung." Naomi turned to her oldest son, "Denny…that is not very nice."

"It is alright Naomi." Turning back to the boys who were just standing there looking at their grandfather, "Boys that is the very first question I had when they told me that they wanted to give me an overhaul. I'll tell you right now it feels kind of weird. I mean I've been hooked up to that oxygen tank for a few years now. Now I've got it in the house but only if I feel I need it."

"What about the new heart, pop?"

"Well son, so far so good. I had to promise I would exercise every day."

"You mean like your neighbor and run every day?"

"No Russell I was told not to overdo it. For right now I just need to take nice leisurely walks."

"OK children let's go inside. I've got a little snack for you guys. I didn't know if you'd be hungry, so there is bread cold cuts and mustard or mayo. Pickles if you want." Myra gave a quizzical look at her son.

"Mom that sounds great."

Myra glanced over at her husband, then to Naomi, "Tomorrow is Easter Sunday, will you be going to mass with us?"

Russ spoke up. Yes mom that sounds great." Putting his arm on Naomi's shoulder, "doesn't it, Naomi?"

Looking directly into his blue eyes, and with very little enthusiasm, "Yeah Russ, that sounds great. Right now after I have a sandwich I am going to crash."

Russell just shrugged his shoulders, "Mom I'm sure she will want to go to church." Myra first glancing at Bryn, then with a hand covering Russell's, "It's alright Russell. You guys have been through hell. I cannot even imagine what it much be like. The worse thing I ever had to worry about with you kids is when you all had the measles at the same time."

Glancing at the little breakfast nook, then a second look. Russell shaking his head, rubbing his red eyes, "Wow! Gray skirt, pink blouse. I never thought you needed make-up, but with what you have on you look great. What you didn't bring you heels; although the black pumps, or are they loafers, look great. Me I had to dig in my suitcase for my cleanest dirty pull over shirt, and slacks that didn't look like there were slept in."

"Well Russ you do what you can with what you got. You want to see how the boys are coming along? By the way Russ if you look in that suit bag you will find a pair of kakis, and a nice button down tan shirt."

Before Russ was able to walk back to the bedroom where the boys spent the night, the boys actually skipped into the kitchen. "Mornin parents."

Looking over at his wife, "Where did you keep those clothes for the boys?"

"Kept them in the suit bag with mine, same place I kept you stuff." Replied Naomi. Bryan's breathing seemed a little labored, "Dad, you doing OK?"

"Well son I've felt worse. Don't know what's going on. Maybe I just need a cup of coffee."

Myra came out in a nice power blue pant suit with her heels in her hand. Studying her son, daughter-in-law and the boys. "Myra you look great, the boys are looking good, but Russell not so good."

"Mom I'm going to change."

Everyone looking at Bryan. Myra asking, "You doing alright, Dad?"

"Yeah Myra. I'm OK now. Don't know what happen."

Surprisingly everyone was ready and they were able to make the 8:00 AM mass. The parking lot at the church was not that crowded. "I do think they may be a problem parking at the 10, and 12 masses. Many of these people only show up twice a year; Christmas, and Easter with the occasional baptism." Commented Myra.

"Sounds a lot like my dad. Seems like the older he's getting the more he attends church. My mom says that that he hasn't missed a Sunday or holy day of obligation mass in the last two years." Replied Naomi.

Myra, and Bryan marched the family down the center aisle to the second pew from the front. The younger Gallagher's would have been quite satisfied somewhere near the rear of the church. Anthony kept looking back at the cry room.

The priest's white vestment trimmed in gold seemed to all but sparkle. Before stepping down from the Ambo, the priest looked into the congregation, *"Haec dies quam fecit Dominus*: "This is the day which the Lord has made." Throughout the octave we shall sing of the unequalled joy which throws open eternity to us. Every Sunday will furnish a reminder of it, and from Sunday to Sunday, from year to year, the Easters of this earth will lead us to that blessed day on which Christ has promised that He will come again with glory to take us with Him into the kingdom of His Father."

Back at the senior Gallagher's house, Both Denny and Anthony were high-spirited, Bryan and Russ were in an animated conversation, and Myra was busy briskly moving about the kitchen. Naomi appeared sullen and withdrawn.

Noticing Naomi with a full cup of coffee, making no attempt at drinking the coffee, "Naomi what's the matter. "Oh, Russ today is supposed to be what it's all about, I mean we celebrate the Resurrection. Everything is supposed to be roses. I just can't celebrate when I don't know what is happening to my baby. I don't know where she is. If she is being hurt. Oh Russ I don't know if I can handle much more."

Myra ran cold water over her hands from the kitchen sink and wiped them with one of the dishtowels. Glancing back at Naomi, "I know, it's not very sanitary but in fifty years of marriage I don't think Bryan or Russell ever got sick from anything in my kitchen; that includes me."

Wiping her eyes with the back of her knuckles, "Oh Myra it is not you or your home. I miss my baby. We will be leaving early tomorrow, and I honestly have to tell you that I'm going to miss your home, and this house. You and Bryan too. Bryan gave me a little scare this morning. But it looks like Bryan is doing much better. I see the two men have found something to disagree on; probably sports."

Myra gazed over at Naomi, then lifting her head, "You know I was envious of you and Russ."

"Myra, why in the world would you be envious of us. You and Bryan seem to have it all together."

"Well Naomi, one thing you and Russ have a wonderful family. God never saw fit to bless me with more than one child. Don't get me wrong. Bryan has been a wonderful husband. Sometimes I wished he would have been more demonstrative. You know it would have been nice to get the occasional hug; even in public. But you guys..."

"I'm just going to let the kids work off some of that energy that includes the big kid; you know your son."

"Are you going to try and drive straight through?" Asked Myra.

"You know I know better than to push myself on the road, but with everything that has happened I'm just a little shell shocked about stopping any place. Russ and I can take turns driving, but there are things a body needs to do, so I'm sure we will be stopping."***

A couple of roadside rest area stops and several hamburger and the Gallagher's where pulling into the drive in St. Pete.

"Denny, think you can give me a hand with some of this luggage?"

"Give me a minute, Dad. I really gotta pee." Replied Denny. Anthony standing next to Russell, and looking up, "I can help."

Dumping the dirty clothes out next to the washing machine. Denny, and Anthony were spread out in front of the TV. Russell with a glass of iced tea in his hand was reclined in his recliner, when Naomi caught the full glass of tea just before Russ was about to let the glass fall out of his hand. Naomi went into the laundry room and put the dirty clothes in the washing machine, and just closed the lid.

Standing in the middle of the living room and taking in the sight of her sleeping family, "Alright everybody! Who wants food?" No answer. "Then let us all retire to our beds." Both boys rubbing their eyes. Russell yawning and standing up. "Tomorrow is a big day. Dad you need to sign in at the air base, and you boys need to get back to school. I have to check with my boss to see if I still have a job."

Sitting in front of a desk with a very skinny major, Russell is starting to feel like that dog that people used to put in the back window of their car, just to watch the head bounce up and down. It took him a few minutes to realize the major, Major Wiley, the Squadron Commander was actually asking him a question. "Sir?"

"I was saying that I don't think you have filled out this Emergency Data form."

"Sir? Major Wiley. I'm not sure what you mean. I've put down my name and address, my wife's name. The names of my kids. I really don't know what else you want."

"I'm sorry Sergeant, but I need your personal e-mail address."

"Sir, I don't own a computer."

Master Sergeant Gallagher, you must be the last person on earth without a computer."

"My wife uses one for work. I'm competent with the use of the programs we use in the Air Force. We used a computer in Fallujah to flight follow. I've used the computer to run the numbers, aircraft times, to monitor metal fatigue, pilot crew rest, we also monitored pilot medical records. To answer your question, once out of the Air Operations Center I just wanted to stay away from the electronic devil."

"Well Mater Sergeant, you need to become so familiar with the new Cyber Air Force that you will be operating a computer n your sleep. Not only that I need you to understand the workings of our new Cyber Air Force. Do you understand Master Sergeant? You know now in the twenty-first century we also keep our publications updated on our computers."

"Yes sir. I assure you I will be current in the use of computers."

"And?"

"I will make sure to get up to date on the cybernetics."

"Thank you. Tech Sergeant Granger is expecting you. He's over at Command and Control. I need you to get up to date as soon as possible."

"Yes Sir."

"By the way I heard rumors that you are dealing with personal problems?"

"Yes sir, my lit..."

"Sergeant I do not want to hear it. You got problems, you leave them at home. Now get out of here."

Russell stood and turned to walk out of the Major's office, "Oh Master Sergeant I meant to ask…"

"Yes sir?"

"What were you job assignments while in the desert?"

"Sir I worked flight management. I made it possible for our flying personnel to stay current and up to date on Air Force publications having to do with flying."

"I do have one more question. How did you get assigned to Command and Control?"

"I am not sure sir, but I will do any job assigned to me to the best of my ability."

"Alright. Check in with Tech Sergeant Granger."

Entering a Building with a sign over a gray metal door, and the words in black over a white sign telling everyone that this is the Command Post Russell noticed a large heavy blond Tech Sergeant. Standing and walking towards Russ with his hand out. "In case you haven't guessed I'm tech Sergeant Granger." Looking down at his protruding belly, "And after 16 years the Air Force has decided that I should find another occupation."

Russ looked directly in the other man's pale blue eyes, "I take it that it wasn't your idea to leave the Air Force."

"Your right, but like I've heard you can't cry over spelt milk."

"I often wondered just what that meant."

"I have no idea."

"Master Sergeant Gallagher, would you like coffee, a soda, maybe a bottle of water?"

"No I'm fine for now."

"I take it you got the big speech about this being a new improved Cyber Air Force. Don't let it scare you. You have some good troops here, and they will help you in any way they can." Clearing is throat and letting out a breath, "They will do anything to keep Wiley Coyote out of here."

"What about during flying ops, or exercises?"

"Well the pilots don't want him around. Our Wing Commander doesn't really want to be around him. So he's given busy work and told to stay in his office. He wears Command Pilot Wings, and is occasionally scheduled to fly the back seat."

"I'm surprised I didn't have to check in with the Wing Commander."

"Oh he's at some kind of conference."

"Just in case anybody ask. What the Wing Commander's name?"

"Sorry bout that. Paris. His name is Paris; Colonel Dwight Paris."

"OK…Let me give you the bus driver's tour." Walking toward a metal door with a sign written in English, and Spanish was the words that Deadly Force will be used on any unauthorized person entering this room.

"One other thing, Russ."

Scratching his head, "OK, Cyrus, what is that thing?"

"Our job description. You're an Operations Specialist, I'm a Command and Control Supervisor. Our job is unique…."

"OK. Please go on. We not only to babysit pilots, and typical air crews. We also take care of other command and control specialist. If you hadn't noticed we fly AWACS, and we have Command and Control and Radar Specialist airborne."

Opening the door Russ felt as if he were entering a movie theater. The lights were down there was subdued lighting behind a white board that was above a little raised platform it looked to Russ like a little stage. On entering the room Russ noticed a red phone with no button or dial, at the end of the console near the entrance. The other two positions had audio jacks where head phones could be plugged in. to the left and behind the console was a glassed in room with audio jacks for head phones. On the far end of the console inside the glassed in room with another console was a digital phone. In the middle of the console was a radio, with both VHF, UHF, an ultrahigh frequencies, next to that radio was another radio. CYRUS explained, "This is our secure radio. Every day a different code is entered into the radio; sometimes several times a day. It works with the aircraft radios by constantly changing frequencies. Supposed to keep the bad guys from intercepting our pilots' radio calls." Pointing to each end of the console CYRUS, remarked, "We also have a flight strip holders."

There was an office on the far end of the Command Post. Sergeant Granger motioned for Russ to follow him. He was standing in front of a desk with a standard size desk top computer with a 21inch monitor on a moveable shelf that went under the desk. The computer was also under the desk, but set back; apparently so someone could sit at the desk without cracking their shins. There was another desk with a normal sized desktop computer with a printer beside it. "OK Russ. You don't mind if I call you Russ do you?"

"Only if you let me call you Cyrus

"Sorry, my mother used to call me Cyrus." With a chuckle, "Just call me Cyrus, or if the brass is around call me Tech Sergeant Granger. Now let me explain the computers. The computers in the Command Post are secure, and on the Air Force secure line. As we entered the office the first computer is set up on the worldwide web. The one next to the printer is used like Quick Books. We can create spread sheets. We also use that one for schedules, and can be used like a word program. The servers for the secure computers are in that room next to the office.

"OK, I got it." Looking for at least a little smile, "You know I have no idea what you just told me. I may be calling you from the gate just to find my way out of here."

"You'll be fine. Airman Wills, our admen specialist, will be in tomorrow. Staff Sergeant Jones is the duty controller tomorrow. Either one of those guys can help you navigate our... What is it our leader calls it? Oh yeah. Our Cyber Air Force. I'm off for the next two days. But just in case I'll give you my personal phone number."

Crossing the Gandy Bridge Russ was trying to organize his thoughts, thinking about his first day at his new assignment. *Not much different than the many first days I had in the many schools I attended growing up. That is until my dad retired and I actually started high school and finished in the same school. And no matter what duty station there was always someone that seemed to go out of their way to make things difficult. The one thought that always helped was the fact that people in the military still get transferred. Why was I assigned to the Command Post? I'd heard of people in the Army being assigned out of their designated job codes. Unless the Air Force is getting desperate for bodies. I've been in Air Operations and Flight Management for over ten years. In all these years I never once wondered about those AWACS people.*

He had spaced out, as the kids would say, so as he reached the summit of the bridge the sun hit his eyes. He reached for the sun blinds, pulled down his sun glasses, when he noticed the sun reflecting off a car on the far side of the bridge. Squinting into the sun he caught a glimpse of a light rack on the roof of the car. Looking down at his speedometer, "Shit," the needle of the speedometer was at 90 miles an hour. Gently tapping his breaks he managed to bring the car down to 60 miles. Passing the police officer he heard the quick short blast of a siren. Looking back it didn't look as if he was following him. *That is all I need. Finding out the job description of the job I'm expected to do is as clear as mud. Learning about computers other than how to turn them on, write reports, checking the weather and flight following. Cyrus Granger mentioned code; whatever that means.*

Pulling into the driveway and Naomi coming to the door with a smile, the kids in a better than normal mood. "Good evening Gallagher family. You guys seem to be in unusually good spirits."

"Well husband it was not all bad. The boys got a ride in a taxicab this morning; so did I by the way."

Putting his hand under Naomi's chin, "I'm so sorry. We need to see about getting a second car."

"It's OK, Russ. There is no real hurry. Nancy, an attorney I work with will pick me up and take the boys to school and me to work. She's a partner in the firm so she pretty much runs her own hours. Won't last for long, but maybe long enough to acquire another car."

After six weeks and several headaches while reading the Command Post manuals, procedures, and specific rules and regulations he was finally beginning to understand the operation of command and control. In short the command post was to act as the eyes and ears of the Commander.

Colonel Paris had returned from his conference at the Southeast Sector located at Tyndall. Russell was spending more time with the Wing Commander then he was comfortable with. The colonel was more than patient with Russell.

He was starting to spend more time in his office at Command and Control. He was used to taking off for lunch, and either eating at what used to be an NCO Club but was now called the Enlisted Club. Russ was pondering to himself, *"I was excited when I became an NCO. I enjoyed the recognition and special privileges of being a Non-Commissioned-Officer. Now to be politically correct everyone is treated the same.*

This morning Naomi had made him tuna salad sandwiches. He had gone to the coffee lounge to eat, but thought that if he brought his coffee back to his office he could work on bringing the pubs up to date and working on the controller schedules as one of the controllers was due to go on leave.

Walking into the office he was aware that Airman Wills was just about glued to his computer monitor. Looking over his shoulder, he was surprised to see the airman watching hard core porn. Noisily clearing is throat, and tapping Wills on the shoulder, "Airman! Just what are you doing?"

"Hey Sarge, have you ever seen anything like this?"

"I'm not a prude Airman, but I really don't think you are allowed to do that on duty."

"This is my lunch break."

"Aren't you comprising the computer system?"

"No, this computer is not hooked up to the Air Force Net or the base net."

"Airman I don't want to see that in here again."

"Whatever."

Russ took his coffee and his sandwich and went back to the coffee lounge. Thinking, *now I know why I have never had a computer in my house.*

It was still very hard to focus on a job for Russ and for Naomi. The wonder the pain in the pit of Naomi's stomach. For Russ it wasn't much different. He liked an occasional beer and on occasion a scotch, but the beer was becoming daily. A weekend didn't go by that he did not finish a bottle of scotch.

It was a Saturday morning when the phone rang. Russ was already on his third scotch when Naomi picked up the phone, "Naomi, this is Asa."

"Asa?"

"Yes, Special Agent Asa Williams. Is Russ near?"

"Yes, Yes. Have you found Jackie?"

"Sorry. I just wanted to check in with you, and let you know that we have not forgotten about you or your little girl."

"I'm putting the phone on speaker." Turning to Russ whose eyelids were half closed and his empty glass was just about to fall out of his hand. "Russ, its Agent Williams."

His head popping up, "Have they found our baby?"

"No."

"Listen Russ has the Agent there in Tampa been keeping in contact with you?"

"I don't even know his name, but the FBI did call about half a dozen times. Has anybody found anything about our child?"

"I am so sorry. I do want to assure you that Tom and I have not forgotten about you, and anything that has come through. We have had a few promising leads."

"Asa, it is becoming all I can do just to stay focused. My life is falling apart. I can't concentrate. And believe it or not I'm much better off than my wife. I can tell the boys are having their own problems. Their grades have dropped. Anthony doesn't go outside much, but he does have his friends, which I no longer see. I think he tells them to just stay away. Denny is doing a little better. You know I think the worse part for all of us is the not knowing."

"Russell, I can only imagine what you are going through but I still think we have a better than good chance of getting your little girl. There has been a lot of activity on the Crow Reservation. It doesn't sound so good for them, but several more young girls have come up missing, Young women too."

"That doesn't sound good at all."

"I feel it means that Jackie still alive. I don't believe she has been harmed?"

"Why. Why Asa. We have not been contacted to money. I'm only a Master Sergeant in the Air Force. I suppose someone might think I have access to government secrets. I don't. So why my little girl?"

"I have a few thoughts. Just don't you give up hope?"

"Thanks Asa. I beginning to feel that our case has been put at the bottom a very large stack."

"If it is any consolation, I have not stuck your case on the bottom of a large stack. Even when they try to take me off the case, or assign me additional work. Jackie is the first person I think of when I wake up and the last person I think of before I collapse at night. I gotta go now. I may be coming your way soon. Good-by Russell, I will be seeing you soon."

Walking out of the bedroom Naomi stopped when she noticed Anthony sitting on the couch, "Anthony what are you doing? You gave me a fright. I didn't know you were there." Looking in his lap she noticed a rather thick hard covered book, "What are you reading?"

Looking up at his mother, "I'm sorry I found this book on the book shelf in your bedroom. Right now I'm reading about Padre Pio."

That's OK. You can read it, but I think you need to get closer to the light."

"I was fraid that you would be mad caus I went into your room. I heard you and dad talking on the phone. Was that the FBI man?"

"Yes Anthony. He just wanted to let me know that he was still on the case. He thinks he knows where she might be."

"I know where she is," He looked up at his mom. He could see that her face was getting red. "But mommy, I do know."

"Anthony stop that. There is nothing about your sister being missing that is funny or cute. Even if this invisible friend of yours told you." With her hands on her hips, "Anthony I know you miss your sister but I am really starting to get mad at you. I really don't need you making up stories."

"Sorry." Opening his book where his finger was. *She's my sister. I know where she is.*

I'm almost 8-years-old. Nobody will listen to me.

Chapter 14

Sam Whitehorse could not pick a better time for is mini vacation. He and Ride the Horse had received suspensions. Nathan said that they should have been fired. The only thing that came to Sam's mind was, *it's a good thing there are not that many people that actually would like being part of the Tribal Police.*

It wasn't a bad time to be on vacation. Summer in Montana is great. He was sitting on the little metal steps leading up to his single wide trailer. Comments had been made about his home. Like if any more rust spread on his home he'd be enjoying the rising sun. He really didn't think that was all that bad a thing to happen. His grandfather would not die until his grandmother called the family together and move him outside.

He had a can of warm beer. On the can was comment that it was locally brewed. Sam's taste were not that discerning, but if he had anything to do with brewing that beer he sure wouldn't tell anyone. The door to the trailer was shut, but he thought he heard his house phone ringing. He had a cell phone; it was on his dresser. The ringing stopped. No it started up again. "Ah," dragging himself up the steps and into the oven that was his trailer. By the time he picked the receiver up the ringing stopped. Opening up windows; at least the ones that he could open. A few of the windows were stuck closed. He had been meaning to work them lose, or break them.

He was heading for the room he used as a bedroom; the one where he left his cell phone when the phone started ringing again. Picking up the receiver, "Yeah, this is Whitehorse."

"Whitehorse is that the way you talk to your boss. Of hell is that the way you were taught to talk to your elders."

"Nathan, I still have a week left of my suspension."

"I know. I need you to come in. I've been trying to reach Ride the Horse; no answer. Nobody has seen him. If you could get hold of him I'd like him to come in."

"Lieutenant, I haven't been near the station. So whatever happened it wasn't me."

"Sam you've done your time and you are not in trouble. Paula's teenaged daughter is missing, so is Little Tree's daughter. They're both teenagers. Now Paula's kid has been a handful, but Little Trees, daughter has always been a good kid."

"How old are they?"

"They're both 16. If they had only been missing for a day or so I would think they just ran off with their boyfriends. Ellen doesn't have a boyfriend."

"I think I know where Robert is. He likes to go into the mountains. He is very hard to find, but when we were boys I tracked him to his favorite trout fishing spring. He used to set up a lean-to, but not too long ago he talked about building a cabin." Replied Sam.

"Sam get in here as soon as you can. You're to partner up with Ride the Horse."

"Nathan, I would rather do it myself. I don't need a partner. I mean we're looking for missing kids. Right?"

"Got a feeling, Sam. You know that little girl came through here, and was taken right from under our protection. This is not the first time people have been missing from the Rez, but I got a feeling."

"OK, Nathan. I'll stop by before I head for the hills. If Ride The horse is where I think he is…"

"Yes, go on."

"It's a two hour drive and then another hour walk."

On the road out of Woodland Park Colorado Darlene reached over and grabbed Melvin arm, "Melvin, Melvin, look at me."

"Darlene you want me to drive off this mountain? What do you want?"

"I don't like this van. I liked the van we had."

"If they haven't I sure they will be looking for the old van. Besides this van does not have any rust, and it drives real good. We got to go back to Montana."

"I thought we couldn't go back."

"I no sooner charged the cell phone and it started playing that damn music. It was vibrating all over the dresser. Larry has a job for us."

"Melvin. I don't like that Larry guy."

"Well get over it. We need to go back to the Rez. There's a package for us. It has already been rapped. I understand the package is real quiet."

"Is it going to be like picking up that little baby? The last time I saw that baby she was in the hospital."

"We're picking up two stoned teenage girls."

"Melvin if the cops sees us we will be arrested."

"We won't be there that long, and besides they're not lookin for a Caravan.

Coming onto the highway heading for Colorado Springs. Melvin pulled the van off the highway and into to a small residential area. Finding a little park he parked the van and stepped out walking over to a small ledge overlooking the highway.

Darlene opened the passage side door. Looking over at Melvin, "What are we doing here? Melvin there are clouds below us."

Opening the door and stepping out, Melvin took several deep breaths, "Darlene come on step out here and breathe some of this rarefied air. We **should** be able to see clouds below us. We are seven thousand feet above sea level."

Looking down on Pikes Peak Highway, then carefully walking around the van to stand next to Melvin, "I thought you said we needed money, and your friend wanted you to pick up these kids right away."

"As usual you are right, but we have enough money to get to Montana, and the girls, from what he told me, are resting."

"They are teenagers, they won't be resting long."

"I don't know exactly what they were given, but they will be in La La land for a while."

"OK, Melvin. Where do we take them?"

"We will be told when we get there. There is cash waiting for us when we get back to Montana."

"Well, Darlene, I think we must be getting on our way. I wonder if it would be safe to go back to our place."

"Melvin, I always let you do what you think is best, and I sure could use some of my stuff. No I don't think we should go anywhere near Lodge Grass."

"From what Larry told me we don't need to go anywhere near Lodge Grass or Agency. The girls are being held in Helena."

"Melvin, our old van had a closed in cargo area, no windows. This minivan has windows. Windows from the front to the back. We had enough trouble trying to hide hat 3-year-old."

"First Darlene, this is not a minivan, it's a Caravan. From what Larry told me these kids will be drugged. They spent a couple of days drinking beer and smoken dope. Youi know Larry is a real doctor. Once the kids got real high he gave them both a shot, and a pill. He told me they would be awake but would do whatever they were told, plus they won't remember anything. All the windows on the Caravan I had darkened; at least as much as the law in most states allow"

Raising her eyebrows, "Never heard of anything like that."

"What if we get stopped?"

"We'll make it like a game they will do what we say whatever we tell them to."

From the tree line Sam was watching Robert; in water up to his waist wearing rubber waders, a red flannel shirt, and trying to fly fish like a white man. Moving stealthily from the tree line down to the edge of the water. "Brother Ride The Horse, does that work better than the way our fathers taught us?"

Almost falling in the cold spring water, "Whitehorse, what are you doing up here?"

"Nathan needs us."

"I'm on suspension, and why does he need both of us?"

"I asked him the same question. I was sitting on my door steps with a cold brew, just pondering the Big Sky when he disturbed me. Seems like someone is weeding out our tribe. Little Trees' daughter, and her daughter's friend are missing."

"The other girls wouldn't be Paula's?"

"How did you guess?"

"They both probably ran off with their boyfriends. They'll show up."

"I don't think so. Not this time anyway. I mean before I came up here I checked out all the spots the kids like to hang out."

"One last cast."

The fly barely hit the surface of the surging waters when a large jumped right on the hook. Throwing the trout in the small wicker basket hanging from a leather strap around his neck, "You want to share him? Got a little fire right around the bend. Of course we could always throe him back."

"Why not some of this fish? Don't take that long to cook. Maybe that white man has something with that fly fishen."

Pushing his long black hair over his shoulders, and tying it back with a piece of line. "It looked like you were enjoying what you were doing."

"Beats the hell out of staring at four walls."

Sam and Robert were standing in front of the old splintered desk when Nathan Green, Lieutenant Nathan Green looked up from a large pile of crime reports. Sam looked down and noticed they were all of missing girls, some women from Agency, and Lodge Grass. Nathan reached to the side of the desk and handed two Missing Child Reports to Sam. "I see you guys making faces at my old splintered desk, but this old maple splintered desk was here long before I went off to Vietnam, and from what I've been told one of the first Tribal Police Chiefs sat behind this desk."

Ride The Horse spoke up, "Sorry Chief."

"How many times do I have to tell you not to call me Chief, besides unless you know something I don't know, I'm still police lieutenant. Now I want the both of you to talked with Ellen's mother, Paula, and Sarah's mother, Mary Little Tree. I called down to the school and talked with the principal. He says they are both good kids, although Sarah is starting to notice boys. Ellen is a pretty thing but has not found any one boy that interesting; at least not yet. Her mom says she spends most of her time studying or playing soccer. I need you two to find out where the kids go and who knows them, besides the kids in school."

Paula was a single mother. Ellen had a brother, no one in the house had seen the father. The last Paula hear he was in jail. That was five years ago. She did know that he had been released, but had no idea where he could be.

Sam was sitting on a worn couch in Paula's double wide with his Stetson on his lap. Scratching his head he looked over at Paula, "Do you think Ellen has had any contact with her father?"

"Listen Sam I know how kids are today, but Ellen has never even asked about her father. She hasn't mentioned him one way or another. I never bad mothed him, so I think if she had seen him she would tell me."

"Well just to cover everything. What is his name?"

"His name is Joseph. He's a tall man with a scar under his lower lip. It almost makes a person think that he has two bottom lips. His name is Joseph Mitchell. His people live up near Yellowstone. I called up there, but they had no idea where he was. Sounded like they didn't want to know."

Paula do you mind if we look in Ellen's room?"

"Yeah go ahead."

Sarah's mother, Mary Little Tree, was wiping her hands on a dish towel when Robert and Sam knocked on the door of a modest well-kept stucco three bedroom house. Sarah's dad died five years ago. He was working in the minds, and was crushed when the mine collapsed. Sometimes he was away for a month maybe longer. Then one day a white man in a nice gray suite came and told me he was dead. He left us some insurance, but I still had to go to work. Sarah is a good kid. She wants to go to college. She was hoping for a scholarship. I did smell beer on her breath, but that was last year. She told me she didn't like it, and wouldn't do it again."

"Mary, would it be alright if we looked in Sarah's room?"

On the streets Robert and Sam found out that the two girls were friends. Seemed that whatever one did the other had to do. They competed with everything; in school for grades and on the soccer field. Neither one had a reputation either with boys or drinking.

"Sam I know we don't have jurisdiction off the Rez, but I know a place in Billings where kids like to hang out. Why don't we take a little ride into Billings?"

"What is that, about another twenty minutes? Why not."

"By the way Sam."

"What?"

"Your pocket is buzzing."

Holding the cell phone out away from his face and closer to Robert; who was driving. "Yeah Nathan I hear you. I wondered when you would suggest that. We got a hunch, and we're heading for Billings."

Robert glanced at Sam, "Well. What did he say?"

"Said he would call the local police let them know we are coming. He also said he wants us out of uniform."

"Shit, this is all I got. I ain't got nothing but a thread bare pair of jeans, and a sweat shirt."

Sam just shook his head, "What did you wear on your date the other night?"

"My uniform. I just took the badge off."

"Well, Ride The Horse, the lieutenant wants us out of anything that would say that we were part of the Tribal Police."

Rubbing his eyes, "We need to go back to Agency so we can change. I think I might have something at the trailer that just might fit you. I have some clothes that I haven't been able to wear. It has been about four inches ago."

"That's great Sam, but you are taller than me."

"They're jeans and you can roll them up."

Chapter 15

A few miles outside Billings Melvin pulled the Dodge Caravan of the blacktop and onto a gravel dusty narrow road, and then on a dirt road that looked more like a cow path. Smacking Darlene on the knee, "See the log lean to. Looks like where they might heard wild pigs. Well Larry said they would be here."

Scooting up in her seat, "Melvin there ain't no people over there."

"Let's get a little closer."

Sure enough looking into the darkened log shed, Melvin noticed movement. Climbing out of the Caravan, and sticking is head in the darkened space inside the log shed, "Yow! Anybody in there?"

Just then he heard giggling. "I hear somebody back there. Larry sent us."

An old raggedy looking white man with an untrimmed looking gray specked brown beard, yellow fingernails, and yellowed blood-shot eyes came to the entrance to the log shed, coming to the entrance and squinting into the sun, looking up at Melvin. OK. So you're here. Are you ready to transport these two?"

"Larry said you'd have some money for us, and an address."

The old guy, spoke, more like croaked, "Don't know notten about money. You're going to Chicago."

"Well friend I ain't goen no place without money."

"Maybe I can give you a few dollars."

"Well friend. You want for Larry to pay you? You give us enough money to get to where he is. The way I figure it I don't get my travel pay, you don't get paid."

"I don't got no money. That little Arab said you had the money."

"Guess what? You get to keep the kids."

After the bearded man pulled out a roll of bills, pulling off eight twenties and four fifties, "OK. I don't need this. When you see your little Arab Doctor tell him not to try and get in touch with me again."

Darlene standing directly behind Melvin kept slapping him on his back, "Melvin where are these kids? I don't hear any kids."

Putting both his hands on the bearded man's shoulders, "You heard the lady where are the kids?"

Turning his head toward the darkness of the shed, "OK, sweeties, it is time for you to take a little trip."

One of the girls spoke like she had just woke up, "Is somebody gona take us to West Wick Lane in Billings?"

The old bearded man got right into Melvin's face, "OK my lovelies your chauffer is here."

Melvin stepped back several feet; this old man's breath smelled of decaying food or something dead. It was about to knock him out. "I thought there was two girls?"

"There is. Neither girl is feeling any pain. Chances are they'll sleep all the way to Chicago. If they do get restless I've got a couple of these here, patches that the rag-head doctor gave me. Already put a patch on each girl. I'll give you a few more you can use ifen they get restless."

Darlene was staring at the baggies with the patches, "What are they?"

"Doc said the patches are Fentanyl; they're supposed to be like morphine, only the patches go into the blood stream a lot slower than a shot or a pill."

"You know Melvin, it's weird."

"What's that?"

"Oh, you know we carried that little girl for a week, and even when she was sleeping I knew she was there. We got two teenaged girls, and they haven't made a sound. I mean teenaged girls are always giggling. They got that thing that makes them scream a lot."

"There is a rest stop just up ahead. I don't see any cars. I'll stop. Need to stretch my legs anyway. You go back there and make sure they ain't dead, or maybe in some kind of coma."

"OK. How much longer to Chicago?"

"Well it's over a thousand miles. If we drive straight through it should take bout fifteen hours."

"Melvin can you drive that long. Maybe we should stop for coffee or sumthin?"

"As long as we got those kids we won't be stopping. Sept maybe to pee. I guess we could switch out on the driven. Just thinkin, maybe one of us could go into a store and get coffee."

Pulling the caravan onto the gravel on the shoulder of the road and riding the shoulder of the road to the entrance to the rest area, Melvin heard a moan from the back of the Caravan. "Darlene did you hear that?"

"What?"

"I think one of the kids is awake."

Both girls were sitting up when Darlene slid the door open. "You girls need a drink of water. Maybe go pee?"

"Yeah I could use some water. How come it is taking so long to get home?"

Handing a bottle of water to the girls, and then taking the bottle back, "Oh there was a bad wreck, and we had to wait for them to clear the road."

The smaller of the two girls the one that hadn't said anything, "Lady I feel funny. Can't seem to keep my eyes open." Turning to her friend she noticed that she was sleeping, and then the smaller one nodded and her head fell on her chest; her breathing became deep and heavy and she was asleep.

Pulling a map out of the glove box, taking it out of the Caravan and unfolding it.

Attempting to spread the map, finally he looked over at Darlene, "Looks like there is other rest stop up ahead. There should be a gas station about five miles up the road. I'll put the gas in and you go get us some coffee."

Back on the road with Darlene driving. Darlene put her head back on the seat head rest; she thought she heard something. There it is again. It sounded a lot like a puppy whimpering. Pulling onto the graveled shoulder of the road, with her head slightly turned she yelled, "What's the problem back there. "Lady, we both really got to pee."

"OK, let me pull off the road." There were a few picnic tables just a few feet up the road. "I'm going to pull off near those picnic tables. You can pee there."

Rubbing is eyes with the back of his knuckles, "What are you doing Darlene?"

"The girls got to pee."

Lowering his voice to almost a whisper, "You get out with them we don't need them to try and run away."

The shorter of the two girls looked up at Darlene, "Lady there is no rest room. Where are we supposed to go? Why is it taking so long to get to Billings?"

Pointing to a boulder near the picnic tables, "Just go behind that rock."

"We're girls. We have to sit to pee."

Darlene lifted her arms and turned her palms up, "You can squat, can't you?"

Both girls went behind the boulder. They moved a few feet from one another, pulled their pants and panties down and fell flat on their butts saturating their panties and pants.

"Lady, Lady." The bigger girl's speech was starting to slur. Both girls stood and staggered back toward Darlene and the Caravan.

"I can't keep calling you hey and hey you. What are your names?"

The larger girl responded. Pointing to her shorter friend, "That is Sarah, and I am..." Just then her head dropped to her chest."

"Woo, I don't know what's happening, but I feel funny and I can't seem to stay awake. I drank beer before but it never did that me. Oh yeah her name is Ellen. That boy gave me some weed. You think that is why I keep nodding off?"

All quiet in the back seat. By the time they reached Kenosha Wisconsin both Melvin and Darlene had stopped at least a dozen times; neither one of the girls stirred.

"Darlene you know this is where all the good beer comes from."

"As we crossed the state line did you see all those cows? You know they make cheese here too." Turning around n her seat, and looking at the girls; they each had their heads on each other's shoulders.

Melvin glancing over at a squirming Darlene. "What you squirming for? You got ants or some other bugs in your britches?"

"Noo...I just never seen anybody sleep like those two. I was getten kind a worried. Sure wouldn't want to see them die on us."

Melvin was quiet, real quiet for several minutes. "Ya know Darlene, I don't think it would bother Larry one way."

Sitting up straight, and rubbing her eyes with her fingers, "What do you mean by that?"

"Just forget I said anything."

Darlene took a deep breath and turned to the window. Melvin couldn't see her face, but by the hesitation in her breathing he knew she was sobbing. "Darlene. Why the tears. You know what we do."

"Melvin I always thought we was taken the kids to new homes. You know rich people that want to empress their friends with kids. Make their friends think that the kids are theirs."

"You know what we do to make money. Some of the little kids are sold to people like pets. The older ones are sometimes used to work in rich people's homes, if they're pretty they can use them on the street."

Chapter 16

Russell was sitting at the little kitchen table with a cup of coffee nuzzled in his hands. Looking at the clock over the kitchen sink, "Oh shit. We have a big exercise today I need to get to the base." Standing he cracked his knee against the table leg, and the cup dropped splashing coffee down his leg and staining his uniform trousers. "Just what I need."

Naomi looking up from the paper, "Calm down Russ. I don't ever remember you being late. So if you're a few minutes late it won't be the end of the world."

His face was getting red. He stopped and took a deep breath, "You know you are right, but this guy I work for is looking for a reason to get rid of me."

After changing his clothes Russ kissed his wife and waved at the boys on the way out. "I shouldn't be too late. You can never tell about these exercises, but they are just checking procedures; mostly my paperwork."

Naomi raised her head from the paper, "You want to take a cup of coffee with you?"

"No Naomi. I do not want to take a cup of anything with me. I think I've had enough caffeine for the week."

Walking into the office Airman Wills had his face buried into his computer screen, "Wills has the old-man been in yet?"

Startled Airman Wills jerked his head up, and attempted to shut down the computer. "No boss. Just you me and the chickens."

Glancing over the airman's shoulder, then stopping and staring at the monitor, "Wills I thought we agreed for you not to do that here."

Spinning his desk chair around to face Russell, "I did. I swear. I just booted it up and this is what came up. You got to see this."

Starting to walk away Russ turned back and stopped; he froze at what he saw on the monitor. "What the hell is that?"

"It's some kinda auction, sept they're auctioning off people. Like what I read about in the history book. You know being black and my folks told me about how my great-Grand-Pa told those stories."

Moving Airman Wills out of his desk chair, Russ couldn't keep his eyes away from the screen. Then he saw it. It was a picture of **his** little girl. "Wills!"

"Yeah! I mean yes Sarge, what is it?"

"How can we find out where this is coming from?"

"I don't know. I guess there's a way to get an IP address, but I ain't that good yet. I think I can copy it and get somebody here that knows how to do it."

Russ pulled his wallet out and dug for a worn piece of paper; it had the number to the FBI. Fighting with the base operator to get an outside line. "Operator I can't get an outside line."

"No sir all the outside lines are down for this exercise."

Taking a deep breath and letting the air out slowly, "Listen this is Master Sergeant Russell Gallagher. I'm the NCOIC of the Command and Control here and this is part of the exercise."

Master Sergeant if you need to get an outside line there is a number you can punch in. If you haven't been given the number you can get it from your supervisor."

Stepping outside the Command Post, and using his wireless phone, then listening to it ring. He finally hears the sound of the phone being answered. Waiting several seconds he heard "FBI." How may I direct your call?"

This is Russell Gallagher. You people are investigating the disappearance of my little girl."

"What Agent may I direct your call?"

"Special Agent Asa Williams was working the case."

After what seemed like an hour; was more likely a few minutes, "Sir there is no Special Agent Asa Williams in this office. Do you have a case number?"

"I'm at work, and all the paperwork to do with my daughters' abduction is at home."

"Sir I thought you said your daughter was missing?"

"Yes that is right. She is missing because she was abducted."

"Who is the lead Agent on the case?"

"I told you, Asa Williams."

"We do not have a Special Agent Asa Williams in this office." Getting frustrated, "His office is in Baton Rouge Louisiana."

"Sir I can give you the number for that office."

"Mam. I was told that there would be an Agent from the Tampa office assigned to my case. I did talk to someone, but I can't remember his name. "

"Please hold sir while I connect with the senior Agent."

Russell was still outside the door to the Command Post on his phone when Major Wiley, Colonel Paris, the ops officer and several other officers arrived. Colonel Paris, and the other officers entered the door. Major Wiley just stood in front of Russ staring.

Major Wiley tapped Russell on the shoulder, "Master Sergeant the exercise is about to begin. We have two Birds ready to launch. You will have to tell whoever that you will get back to them. You do know that I discourage personal calls while here."

"Sir this is a critical phone call. You see my lit..."

"Master Sergeant I told you on your very first day that I don't want to hear about your personal problems."

Just then his he felt vibration in his hand. His cell phone was demanding his attention. "Major Wiley, I really do have to take this call."

Shaking his head the Major started to walk into the Command Post, then stopped and turned, towards Russell, "Master Sergeant Gallagher you will report to me at the finish of this exercise."

Watching the Major turn abruptly and head for the Command Post, Russell heard the click on his cell, as Agent Asa Williams answered the phone. Mr. Gallagher do you have information for us?"

"Yes sir, I just saw a picture of my little girl on the computer."

"Did you get in touch with the agent in charge down there; I believe that would be Agent Zackery Taylor?"

"Sir, nobody seems to know who is in charge down here. To be honest and fair, I did talk to Agent Taylor when I first got back in town."

"Give me your address. Tom and I will fly down there as soon as we get the jet cranked up."

Back in the Command Post he observed people decrypting, and encrypting messages. For the first time he observed the secure radio being used. Every day one of his jobs was to set the frequencies the secure radio; he didn't do it this morning. He was sure someone would be out to let him know of his incompetence.

Walking back in the admin section he tapped Airman Wills, on the shoulder. When Wills turned his head back. "Wills you know that stuff you showed me on the computer?"

"Yeah."

"Could you give me the website and show me how to get it?"

"Listen Sarge, it was an accident that it came up. I really wasn't looking for it. I thought I might find a game."

"You're not in trouble. That little dark haired girl that was on the computer screen is my daughter."

"Are you shitting me?"

"No. I am dead serious. You have to promise you won't tell anyone. I've called the FBI Agent that is trying to get my little girl back. Can you help me?"

"I can do it boss, but I will have to break some serious laws."

Staff Sergeant Jones walked into the office with several folders, making a show of filing them. Then looking up from filing. Looking around the office as if looking for someone. When he was sure there was no one to over hear him, "Hey boss, I hope you don't mind but I put today's code in our secure radio?"

Wiping his forehead, "Jones, you just saved my beacon. Thanks. I owe you." Waking back in the office Airman Wills said, "Master Sergeant. If you don't mind I know somebody who can help you with this."

"I don't want you to get in trouble, but if you want I'll tell the powers to be that I was the one who made you do it."

"Naw. I think I can get it for you. It's what they call the Dark Web. Just let me know when the big-shots start coming around."

Russell's pocket started to vibrate, and that god-awful music started to play. "Master Sergeant Gallagher."

"Listen Mr. Gallagher, Tom and I will be landing at Pinellas Airport in about twenty minutes. You want to give me your home address again. We've got a letter of agreement with Pinellas County, and it just so happens that the air base is part of the federal government and so are we, but we don't really want to ruffle any feathers just yet. I'm going to set up our computers in your house. We can work in tandem with our forensic team in Tampa. Do you have Wi-Fi?"

"I don't even know what that means, but Naomi works on a computer all day, plus she has a lap-top. My boys can probably tear a computer apart and put it back together."

Just then Sergeant Jones stepped out the door and yelled, "Master Sergeant, the brass is looking for you."

Russell stepped into his office to see Major Wiley waiting, "Master Sergeant. What did I tell you about personal calls? Now hand that phone over."

Colonel Paris walked into the office from the command post, and eyeing the major and then Russell, "OK Major. What is going on? If this effects our aircraft I need to know."

Major Wiley scrutinizing Colonel Paris.

"Well Major Wiley what is going on?"

"Sir the very day this airman signed into Wing I told him that anything personal was to stay at home, and I did not want to see his personal cell phone while he is on duty. He has deliberately defied me."

"Get over it Major. Master Sergeant, what is the problem."

"Sir…Colonel, my little girl has been abducted, and the FBI Agent that is in charge of the case thinks he has a lead. He is on his way to my house right now."

The Colonel, observing the Major and then turning to Russell, "Master Sergeant, I want you on leave immediately. Call me if you need my help." Watching Russell scratching his head, "Don't worry Sergeant Gallagher, I can find someone to run your office temporally. You've got a good team in there. I'm sure there is someone up to the task."

"Thank you sir." As Russell was turning to leave he noticed a grimace on Major Wiley's face.

In the parking lot Russ felt a hand on his shoulder. Turning he saw Tech Sergeant Granger bent over with his hands on his knees, making sounds like a locomotive he wanted to speak. Finally after taking a deep breath, "Russ. What's going on?"

"I need to take a leave of absence. I just signed papers requesting Emergency Leave. The Colonel already gave his approval."

"I was at the Personnel office signing that little sheet of paper promising I would not tell anyone any Air Force secrets. All of a sudden the clerk picks up the phone, looks at me with a real strange look on his face. Then says come back later. Colonel Paris wants to see you."

"I am so sorry Cy, but there is a lot going on right now and I need some time to take care of it."

"Hey, I don't mind. Sally is going to be pissed. She has boxes all over the house. She has been packing and throwing things away for a week now."

"My daughter has been abducted. Airman Wills was looking at some website, and I happened to see a picture of my daughter. I have a Special Agent coming in today, but I sure could use some help finding that website?"

"Wills is good, but I am better. Already got a job lined up as an internet technician with an insurance company. They don't expect me for a month."

"You know we never did get together for dinner. Why don't you and Sally come over tonight and I'll introduce you to Special Agent Williams?"

Grabbing his little green memo book, Russ writes his address down, tears out the page and hands it to Cyrus. "Do you need me to draw you a strip map?"

"No I can find it. I've been living off Vista in Tampa for the last three years. We're just a few blocks from Gandy, and you are not that far away. See you about 7 pm?'

"Sounds good. Again I am so sorry about screwing up your life. You know for the first time in over a month I feel like something good is going to happen."

Pulling up in the driveway, and before he could get out of the car Naomi was standing at the car door. "OK. Master Sergeant Gallagher, what is going on? Why are you hoe so early?"

"Me? What about you. Aren't you supposed to be working today?"

"Yeah. The school called me at work. The principal herself called. Seems like Anthony was acting out. So I had Nancy give me a ride. There was only an hour left of school so I brought them both home. OK. I told you my story so you tell me yours."

"Several things happened to me today. First I saw Jacquelyn."

With hazel eyes bigger than he had ever seen, glaring directly into Russell's eyes, "Don't you bullshit me. I am in no mood. Especially when you're talking about my baby."

"No this is no bullshit. I was looking over the shoulder of one of my clerk's and I saw her on the computer screen; I mean it was her. I've already notified the FBI. Cyrus, my sponsor is coming over tonight; he and his wife."

"Russell you drop this on me then you expect me to entertain?"

"No he is really good at computers. He is going to help us track the IP address; whatever that is? I think we can find her."

"OK wise guy. My laptop is in the bedroom, I wouldn't know where to start."

"That's OK Agent Williams is coming over. There is a cyber-forensic team assigned to the Tampa branch of the . FBI."

"Russell I am really starting to get annoyed, hell not annoyed I'm pissed. Will you please tell me what is going on?"

Come on Naomi. The neighbors are starting to stare. Let's go inside. I need a glass of iced tea"

Before entering the kitchen, "Russell no tea until you tell me what is going on, and what does that have to do with you being home in the middle of the day."

"I called Agent Williams and told him what I saw. My clerk says he will try and help but he really only fell into the website by accident. The Colonel told me to go home so I could concentrate on getting my daughter back. First it was going to be Asa and his partner. I called him back and told him what I found out about the website. So he is passing on what I told him to the cyber-forensic team."

Filling a glass with ice and pouring strong sweetened tea over the ice, and handing the glass to Russ, "Well this will certainly give our neighbors something to talk about; not that I care."

"Naomi I do not care either. I want our child back, even if I have to put search lights in our front yard. Asa said the operation will be discrete."

Literally dropping into the recliner, glaring up at Russell, "So the Colonel gave you time off. What 24 hours?"

"No. he told me that I needed to take care of my family and I could take as long as I needed."

Cyrus and Sally Granger arrived about 6 PM. Naomi had sliced cold cuts, sliced cheeses, chips and condiments on the kitchen table. There were two large pitchers of cold tea one sweetened and the other unsweetened with a large ice bucket beside.

Cyrus was a rather large portly blond haired man, while his wife sally was a petite shapely auburn haired woman. She hung onto Cyrus as they sat with their sandwiches in their laps on the living room couch.

At about eight a minivan pulled up in the Gallagher's driveway next to Granger's Jeep Wrangler. Naomi came out to the minivan, "Asa, you know we could be friends under better circumstances." Tom was climbing out of the driver's side. As Tom stood Naomi hugged him.

"Tom. You guys go on in the house. There are sandwich makings and cold tea on the table, ice in the bucket. Tell your friend in the back seat to come on out here."

"Sorry. That's Zackery Taylor. He's my other half; my twin down here in the Sunshine State. No is not the 12th president of the United"

Sticking her head in the door and looking at Zackery in the back seat, "Zackery you don't have to hide in the back seat."

"I'll be right in mam. Just need to make a couple calls."

"Naomi, I see you met my other half. Actually he is Asa's other half, or as Asa likes to say his carbon copy." Commented Tom.

Naomi stopped and turned back to the minivan, "You aren't re...?"

"No mam, as far as I know I am not related to President Zackery Taylor. But I have been told he did own slaves, plus I think he was a white dude." Smiling up at Naomi.

Zak came in with what looked like a leather carrying case. In the case was a lap-top computer. Turning to Naomi, "I don't supposed you have WI-five set up in here?"

"As a matter of fact I do have Wi-five in this house. I'm supposed to work an eight hour day, but there have been times I needed to take my work home."

Back and forth on the phone. Zak's fingers flying across the keyboard of his computer.

Granger suggesting ways to find the Dark Web.

Zak's wireless phone rang. After a few nods and several grunts, Zak looked up, "Asa, Tom, our cyber forensic tem has been tracking that IP address all over the world. We still have not been able to pin it down. Our cyber forensic team seem to think it is located somewhere in Illinois.

Out of the corner Naomi noticed Anthony get up and head for his bedroom. She motioned for Denny to follow him. "Denny make sure your brother is all right. This is a little much for me. As a matter of fact why don't you guys just get your night clothes on and go to bed."

"But Mom, it's early."

"Not really, but just get in bed. I'd tell you to turn the TV on but it may distract the people out here. Maybe you two can find a board game; just promise to be quiet."

A very unenthusiastic, "OK." Responded Denny.

Chapter 17

Sam Whitehorse had his head back and his feet up in his worn leather recliner. His eyes were closed and it would appear the can of beer in his left head was about slide out of his hand and spill the remaining warm beer on the scuffed linoleum floor of is single wide trailer, when his eyes opened with a start as he felt the warmth of a body. Turning his head to the left he saw a young boy. His heart seemed to race. He hadn't realized that he was holding his breath until he inhaled the cool summer air from the open door of his trailer. What he saw was a very pale white haired boy of maybe eight. The boy had his hand on his shoulder. When he felt he could finally speak, he looked into the boy's pale blue eyes, "Are you the one they call the Ghost who walks?"

Grabbing the can of beer before it fell on the floor, "I don't know, but you know my sister. Nobody will listen to me. I know where she is. Someone has to get her soon. Something bad is going to happen."

Taking the warm beer out of Anthony's hand, and putting his feet on the floor and sitting up, "What **do** they call you?"

"I am Anthony, and I am not a ghost. Can you help me help my sister?"

Sam stood up, and tilted his head so he would not hit his ceiling, "Where is your sister?"

She is in a big building. It might have been a factory. The building is near a big lake; Lake Michigan. I think the building is a hospital. There is a sign that says Clinic. I think it says reproductive Services underneath Clinic over two big doors in front, and in the back is a fence and beyond the fence is Lake Michigan. I thought it was the ocean, but I saw another sign that said Lakefront Properties. I'm in the third grade and I can read pretty good."

"Anthony, I need more than that to find this place."

"There was another sign. It was a long word that started with a Wak...I couldn't read the rest but the second word was Illinois."

"I can find that, but if I'm right that is a long way from here."

"Mister Whitehorse we need to hurry. There are all kinds of bad things in that building. Two sleeping teenage girls just came in. one might be dead."

"Anthony. I will get Ride The Horse and we will be there soon. I need you, if you can to keep whoever this is from hurting anybody else. Just don't want yourself hurt. Maybe make noise or something. Do you know how to call the police?"

"Yes of course I do. I'm eight. There are phones upstairs in the offices. I think they still work. I just got to push 911."

"Even if we can get an airplane out of Billings tonight it will still take us several hours. I got a thought. Do you know what a fire alarm box looks like?"

"Yeah...yes sir. One of the kids at my school pulled the alarm; boy did he get in trouble."

"Well you are **not** going to get in trouble. Just don' get caught."

Zak was going through the different websites when Cyrus tapped his on the arm, "I don't really want to interfere, but could I give it a try."

Zak motioned for Cyrus to sit next to him on the couch then handed the lap-top to him. "Knock yourself out. Our team in Tampa is shadowing this computer. So far we've been to Syria, Afghanistan, and a few places I never heard of. Our team over in Tampa is doing maybe a little better. I'm sure they will find our address, but it looks like it will take time."

Asa eyed Naomi, "Mrs. Gallagher our men look exhausted. Do you think you could put on a pot of coffee?"

Within minutes the smell of coffee permeated the house. Asa grabbed the cups that Naomi set out, and calling from the kitchen into the living room, "How do you boys take your coffee. In unison without taking their eyes off the computer screen they answered, "Black and strong." Then they glanced at each other and laughed.

Naomi and Sally cleared the table and invited Special Agent Taylor and Cyrus to bring the laptop to the table where they would be more comfortable and closer to an electrical outlet.

Pulling up close to a set on double doors under a large white sign in large block print were the words 'Clinic' under that were the words, 'Reproductive Services' and under that was in much smaller letters 'Waukegan Illinois'.

Darlene looked back at the girls. Sarah was barely sitting up, Ellen was slumped in the back seat. Darlene opened her door and slid the door to the back seat open. Motioning for Sarah to come out, "Sarah can you help me with your friend?"

"Is she dead? She is awfully cold."

Melvin stepped out of the Caravan just as a large black man pushed the two large doors of the clinic open. With a very loud and deep voice, "Hey! You can't leave that there."

Melvin looked up covering his eyes against the glare of the sun on one of the large picture windows to the right of the doors, "This is a woman's clinic right?"

The big black man was coming closer to the Caravan, "Yeah. You got an appointment?"

"They know we are coming. The doctor told me to bring these people here."

Countered Melvin.

"Well you can't leave that van there." Responded the black man. As big as the black man was he had to look up at Melvin as he approached the van.

"No problem, but you get down here and give us a hand with these girls." Melvin slammed the door to the van, and started walking closer to the black man.

As his eyes seemed to open even wider, "OK, mister. I'll help."

Darlene glanced over at the large man, "Could you get a gurney. I can't carry both these girls."

The black man just stood there looking first at Melvin and then at Darlene. "Yes mam." Melvin looking as if he was about burst a blood vessel in his neck, "Get the gurney and then come back here and help."

Picking Sarah up and cradling her in the crook of his arms, leaving Darlene with Ellen, and calling to the large black man, "Hurry we need to get this girl inside."

Once inside the building and near the two doors that could be pushed open with a sign indicating that only authorized personnel beyond this point, was a short dark man with a surgeon's cap, and paper face mask and a green surgical gown. Pulling his surgical gloves off, "What is all the commotion out here?"

The big black man spoke up, "Doctor! Dr. Labeed these people said you told them to come here."

"Yes. Yes. Put the one on the gurney in the pre-op room and the other one in the room nearest the nurse's station. Have someone clean her up, and put her in bed."

Darlene called after the doctor, "Are you the doctor?" Please help her. I think she is dying."

Pulling down his paper face mask from his nose and mouth, "Woman, bring that gurney over here."

Darlene who was heading for the door that had a sign 'Pre-Op' stopped and turned to face Dr. Labeed. With a whimper, and a sniffle, "Are you talking to me?"

"Yes Woman. Bring her here."

Turning to look for Melvin, and noticing him and a reception desk, and yelling, "Melvin. Melvin I need you."

With a deep breath Labeed scrutinized Darlene, then told her, "Melvin says you are a nurse?"

Darlene replied, "No. I used to work as a nurses aid."

Follow me. Take a gown and paper face mask, put the latex surgical gloves on; you're not allergic to latex, are you?" Glaring at her, and then looking over at Melvin, "Tell this woman to follow me."

Dr. Labeed was motioning for Darlene to stand down by the foot of the operating table and to take the young woman's feet and put them in the stirrups at the foot of the surgical table. And for her to hold her feet. "OK. Now do you know what those instruments" pointing to the table, "are?"

Shaking her head, "Yes."

"Then hand me the little rod."

"What is this doctor?" Teary eyed but with a smirk.

"Woman, are you going to have a problem? Have you never seen blood before?

"What am I supposed to do?"

"Pull her legs apart."

"I'm trying, but she is resisting."

Darlene was finally able to pull her legs apart, exposing the girl's cervix. "Now what?"

"Bring her knees up and put her feet in those stirrups."

"Now what?"

"Do you see those probes on the tray?"

"Yes." Darlene responded.

"Tighten the straps around her ankles, and give me that small probe."

"Aren't you going to use saline?"

"No. that will burn the fetal tissue. We need to keep the fetus alive in order to harvest any viable organs

"Doctor, she is convulsing."

"That is just the little intruder dyeing. It won't last long."

Labeed hollered, "Come over here. The slime on this creature is going to cause me to drop it."

Al-abadi pointed to what looked like a smaller operating table with a basinet. "Just put it in there. Don't drop it. I will need to remove as many organs as possible, and I don't want them to become contaminated."

It was a baby. Darlene tried to place the baby in the basinet, but the baby was squirming. She heard what sounded like a kitten. Than the kitten sound got louder until it was a full blown cry. The child had to be at least a foot long, but it had no eyes.

Dr. Labeed walked abruptly over and puled the child out the basinet and put its head between his hands and squeezed until the head was crushed."

Darlene looked over the doctor, sobbing, "No. No. You just killed that baby."

"Be quiet woman. I need to at least get a kidney." Cutting the stomach and removing an organ. He picked up what looked like a wide mouthed stainless steel thermos. He held the kidney with forceps, and showed it to Darlene. "Beautiful. See how pink that kidney is? Perfect." He put the kidney in the empty thermos and gently poured from another thermos with the words liquid nitrogen into the thermos with the kidney in it. He sealed the container with the kidney in it. You've got to hurry. This organ, and this tissue must be snap frozen within 30 minutes."

Pulling his surgical gloves off throwing them in the small trash can marked Biological waste. Turning sharply and walking over to the deep sink, he washed his hands. "Woman come over here get rid of those gloves. Wash your hands and put on clean gloves."

"I can't do this."

"Well if you want to get paid you **will** do it."

"Doctor, Doctor. The girl! She is moaning. I thought she was dead, but she is moaning. I think she is crying."

"What do you want me to do about it?"

"I think she is dying. Help her?" looking over at the doctor, "Are you really a doctor?"

"Yes, but there are people waiting for these organs. Besides there are girls and young women in much better condition that can be used as domestics to some very wealthy people." With tears welling up in her eyes, "Don't you have a regular nurse?"

"Yes. The woman who is supposed to be my nurse is drunk and won't be in today.

Sitting in an aisle seat on a twin engine propeller driven airplane, Robert Ride The Horse's knuckles were white from the pressure of his hands around the armrests. "You know, Robert there are more accidents in cars than on airplanes. I take that back. In your case there are more accidents on horses than on airplanes." Remarked Sam.

"OK wise guy. When are we going to get up in the air? I've been watching the dust that our propellers are kicking up since we left Billings." Observed Robert.

"Robert, it really isn't that bad." Sitting up straight, and tightening his seat belt. "Says you. As you tighten your seat belt. Sam are you sure there is an airport near Waukegan."

"I hope so. That is where this guy said he was going to take us. If he doesn't Nathan is going to be pissed. I think he robbed petty cash just to get us this far."

"Sam, you told me that we would have to pay our own way. I dug my share of the fare out of my sock drawer. We are going to get paid back for this, aren't we?"

"According to my little CI, we should be able to get our teenagers as well as the little girl that was abducted over at Health Services. When we do that, they will have to justify our getting at least travel money."

Glancing over at Sam, "Oh well. You got to go in the Army. You know I ain't never been no place but the Rez."

Glaring at Robert, Sam queried, "Didn't you spend some time in Lawrence Kansas?"

"Yeah, that was to go to a trade school, but I felt like I was still on the Rez, cept there was people from the desert, the planes. You know Navajo, Comanche, and Hopi. Lot of people from the Dakotas. Just one big reservation."

"You been to Billings?"

"Is that off the Rez?"

"Shut up we are either about to land or the engine is on fire, and we are about to crash." Remarked Sam.

"Ya know Sam. Maybe staying of the Rez ain't all that bad." Responded Robert.

Chapter 18

Anthony was in the building near two large garage doors. He was thinking, *those doors are big enough to back a locomotive in.* He was lost. This did not look the same as it did the first time he was here. *This has to be the place. Jackie should be in a big room. But I don't see any rooms. Before I pull a fire alarm I have to be sure I'm in the right place.*

He found a stairway. There was an elevator beside the stairs. He took the stairs. When he got to the second floor he saw doors that looked like office doors. He checked to see if they were unlocked. Most of the doors were locked he did find one that was unlocked. There was a phone on an old dusty desk. It didn't have push button; it had a dial. He picked up the phone and there was no sound.

He came up to another stairwell. These stairs went down. He heard voices coming from below. He was afraid someone would see him so he slowly creeped down the stairs. At the very bottom he saw a light. Holding himself against the wall he peeked in. he saw two people both dressed like doctors with green gowns and their faces covered with paper masks.

He heard two voices. The one sounded like the doctor he saw in Montana. The other voice was familiar, but he couldn't be sure. There was a phone on a desk not far from the two people dressed like doctors. Mr. Whitehorse told him to forget about the phone. To look for a fire alarm.

First I have to find my sister. That big room I saw has to be close. He waited for the two people dressed green scrubs to leave the room. It seemed like it was taking forever. They finally walked out. There was a door on the far side of the room. It was not near the door the two people in scrubs went through. There was no window in the door so he had to open it a little bit. He didn't see any people but he did see another door, and it sounded like there were machines running in that room. He eased the door open and the sound of machines got louder.

In the middle of the room was a big, very big oven. The loud hissing noise he heard was the sound of the gas jets inside the large oven. A full grown person could fit in that oven. He could see blue flames coming out of the gas pipes; like the gas burners on the stove in the house they used to live in.

There was no one in the room. There was another room. He walked to a room with a single metal door. He tried to open the door. It was unlocked.

In all this sneaking around he could not understand why it was so hard to find his sister. The first time he found her was in a little hospital in Montana. *Why can't I find her?*

The third door he opened he saw his sister. There were the same dozen beds; six on either side. It looked as if the bed had sheets that were almost clean. His sister was in the middle of the room on the side farthest away from him. She had a clear plastic mask on her face, her hands were tied to the bedrails, needles and tubes in both her arms and in her feet.

It looked like there was a tube in her nose.

After looking to see if anybody else was around he carefully went over to his sister. Putting is hand on her arm; her arm felt cold. He then put his hand on her head and bent down to listen to her breathe; she was breathing. She was awake, but not moving. There was a sink beside her bed. It looked like a wash rag. He wet the washcloth and put it on her head. She stirred. He put his hand over her mouth. She started to squirm and fight, until she saw him. He put his finger to his lips; Jackie be quiet.

Now he had to find a fire alarm. He heard people coming. It was that short man and the woman. He could see their faces. *That was the dark man he saw in the hospital in Montana. He remembered the woman. That is the woman with the mousy brown hair that his mom was fighting.*

Anthony hid under his sister's bed. He didn't think those people would ever leave. They finally left. At first he was looking for the fire alarm. Then the more he thought about the more he was sure he had to get his sister out of this room. There were other kids in the room, some just babies, many younger than Jackie. Opening cabinets and drawers he found scissors, scalpels; he knew they were scalpels, and they were sharp. He'd seen them on a doctor show he watched with his mom. He took the scissors and a small box of gauze. He took tape, some was the sticky kind then there was tape that didn't have any stickiness.

He thought he heard someone near the door. He stopped and hid under a different bed. Whoever came in turned around and went out. All the people in the room big kids and little kids. There were babies in incubators; they looked to Anthony like they were in plastic boxes with breathing tubes. The tubes were stuck in the babies like they were in Jackie.

Jackie was in the middle of the room on the side away from the door. He was about to take the needles out, and tube out of her nose. *What if Jackie can't breathe without that tube in her nose? What if she needs the medicine that is coming out of the needles? Oh well I got to get her out of here.*

Jackie started moaning when he pulled the needles out of her arms. When he pulled the tube out of her throat she coughed then gagged, and it looked as if she were about to cry. He thought for sure she was about to throw up. She started to scream. Anthony put his hand over her mouth.

She squirmed and looked up at Anthony, "Antnee, where mommy?"

"Be quiet Jackie. You'll see mommy real soon. Right now you have to stay quiet. Can you walk?" He tried lifting her out of the bed. She was stuck. Looking down he could see that there were straps around her wrist. He couldn't figure out how to untie or unbuckle. He reached in the pocket of his jeans and pulled out the thing with the little sharp blade, and cut the straps. He was surprised in how easily the blade cut the straps.

Jackie was having a hard time walking. Anthony half carried her, and half drag her to the door. Pushing the door open he saw what he had been looking for; the fire alarm box. He thought all he had to do was pull a lever on the alarm box. With this alarm he had to break a glass that was covering the lever. He hit the red box as hard as he could; it did not break. Little Jackie was squirming in his arms. She wiggled out if his grasp, she picked up a metal doorstop and swung her hand with the metal stop in it and hit the glass window. It broke, Anthony pulled the alarm. The screech of the alarm was bloodcurdling. The sprinkler system went off everything was getting wet.

Running to the closest stairwell, Anthony saw a door that was partially open. Squeezing in the door he stepped into a bucket. There was a large metal sink in the room; they were in the janitor's closet. Lifting Jackie up in his arms, and trying to yell over the sound of the alarm, "Jackie you got to stay still and quiet."

Holding her, Anthony could feel her belly tighten and start to convulse. He held her over the big sink. She was throwing up yellow bile. She seemed to calm down He stuck his head out and didn't see anyone. He heard the fire engines outside. Looking out the door the hallway seemed empty. No people, no noise. "Come on Jackie. Do you think you can make it?"

"Antnee, Jackie don't feel good. Jackie wants to go to bed. Jackie want mommy."

"I know but we got to get out of here first."

Keeping close to the wall Anthony and Jackie were slowly making their way down the hall, when out of nowhere there was a very large black man coming right at them. The alarm was stopped, but the black man's voice was deep and loud. "You kids stop! What are you doing here? Stop!"

Anthony had no idea where he was going. He grabbed Jackie, half carrying half dragging he ran with his sister. He ran away from the big man. The man that was chasing them reminded Anthony of one of the big football players he had seen. Anthony never knew how really big the football players were until his dad, took him and Denny to a stadium to watch a football game.

It looked like a narrow hallway going off to the right. If he could make it to the hallway maybe he could find a place to hide. Pulling at a door at the end of the hallway he saw what looked like a kitchen. It was the back door to an old cafeteria. There were dusty trays, and an old steam table. There was a big gas stove, a grill, and next to the grill was an oven with two oven doors one on top of the other. The stove and grill were still warm. Somebody cooked food here.

On the side farthest away from Anthony and Jackie was what looked to Anthony like a walk-in cooler. Anthony carried Jackie to the cooler. He thought he heard the man coming. He wasn't sure whether the heavy breathing he heard was him or the big black man. They made it to the walk-in cooler. Anthony felt a rush of cool air as he pulled the door open. There were metal shelves inside the cooler on both sides. On the shelves were Styrofoam coolers. He pulled the top of one of the coolers open. In the cooler was several blue plastic bags of dry ice. At the end near anther refrigerator door on the second shelf was three stainless steel wide mouth thermoses. "Antnee, Jackie thirsty." She reached for one of the stainless steel thermoses on the second shelf. "Me want a drink."

Anthony picked up the thermos; it was so cold that it felt like his hand was burning. With some effort he managed to unscrew the lid of the thermos. He put the opened thermos up to his nose, and took a whiff. Whatever it was gagged him. "**No,** Jackie. We have to wait. Right now we have to hide."

There was another refrigerator door at the back of the walk-in. When Anthony pulled it open all the shelves were covered with snow. "Jackie, let's try and be quiet. We can stand her by the door. Maybe we can find room on one of the bottom shelves."

After coming to a bumpy stop, watching smoke and flames come from each of the two propellers, and the smell of burnt rubber as the pilot must have been checking out his breaks. The sound of the engines changed from a steady drone to a high pitch whine as the propellers were feathered just as they pulled into what must have been there assigned parking place.

Sam cracked his head as he went through the door to what was supposed to be the terminal. Putting his Stetson on and then taking it off abruptly, "Ow."

Cocking his head then looking up at his friend, "OK Kemosabe, what now?" Probed Robert.

"What?" with raised eyebrow, questioned Sam?

Glancing at Sam, "At your age, and you never saw the Lone Ranger?"

"Unlike you, Robert, the first time I saw a TV was when I went in the Army."

"You do know there is more than one movie theater in Billings. The Lone Ranger is a movie now." Commented Robert.

"Nathan gave me a letter to take to the local police." Sam Stated as he pulled an envelope out of his shirt pocket, and taped it.

"OK. I give up. You're taking a letter to the locale police."

"It's to inform the locals who we are and why we are here. Now what we have to do is find transportation." Replied Sam.

Looking around the terminal, Robert spotted a counter with what appeared to be a man sitting at a desk behind the counter. His back was to them but it appeared his head was down on the desk. There was a sign over his head that indicated that they could rent a car.

Robert walked ahead of Sam to the counter where he saw a little bell, he tapped it and watched the man's head pop up, like a turtle sticking his head out of its shell.

The man sitting behind a desk stood up and approached the counter, "May I help you?" With both his hands on the counter, Robert replied, "Yes we need transportation and directions."

"I'm sure I can provide transportation, and if I can't tell you how to get where you need to be I do have maps."

Moving up beside Robert, Sam pulled out his tribal issued credit card. Handing it to the clerk, "I've been told I'm long legged. Is there a full size car available?"

The clerk staring at the credit card, then looking up at Sam. "You Sam Whitehorse?" Sam taking his Stetson off and setting it on the counter, "Yes sir. Is there a problem?"

"No sir. Just never seen an official tribal Master Card."

"Well we are both here on official business, and we need directions to the Waukegan Police Department. I guess the Sheriff is the head law enforcement authority. So how do we get to the Sheriff's Office?" Enquired Sam.

"That's easy. The Lake County Sheriff is down on Martin Luther in Waukegan."

After spending over an hour at the Sheriff's office, Robert and Sam were directed to the Waukegan Police Department, where after explaining several times to several police officers and finally a person in plain clothes what they wanted to do, Sam was handed a form to fill out requesting a warrant. Filling in all the blanks on the form the final bit of information asked for was reason and evidence to request a Warrant.

Entering a small office with frosted glass in the door, and speaking to an attractive blond haired woman in a nice looking pant suit, "You say that two teenage girls, and a 3-year-old girl are being held against their will by this Al-abadi? No Mr. Whitehorse."

"It's Sergeant Whitehorse, or just call me Sam." Leaning slightly forward, and looking at her name tag, "Ms. Whitmore."

The attractive Ms. Whitmore replied, "As I was saying, Sergeant Whitehorse. I need something to take to a judge. I don't know how you police on the reservation do it, but here we need at the very least Probable Cause in order for me, or anyone else to authorize you to go on private property. You bring me something I can use and I will not only get your warrant but I will take my team and go with you."

"Can you at least tell us where this Women's Clinic is?" Inquired Robert.

"At the old train station you go over the train tracks and it is near the lake. There used to be several warehouses, and manufacturing plants down there. Now there is a housing development down near the lake. The clinic is located right on Lake Michigan. Before you even think of going there you remember that if you enter that facility without permission you will be arrested."

Traveling down the streets of Waukegan Robert points towards a gutted out building. That has to be the old train station. "Sam I think that's the tracks that everybody is talking about. Can't even imagine a train running over those tracks. Didn't she say we're supposed to cross the tracks and go down that little hill?"

"Yeah." The sounds of sirens and about four fire engines heading across the tracks. Drew Sam's attention. "Well Robert I do believe that if we follow the circus we will find the elusive Women's Reproductive Clinic."

The red fire Marshal's car the two of the four fire engines blocked the entrance to the clinic. There were people; mostly women in front of the building.

Robert was the first to notice a dark blue Crown Victoria idling behind them. "Sam look to your left. Those men standing outside the Crown Vic? Isn't that Special Agent Williams?"

"I know my eyes are getting old, but I think you are right."

Looking around Asa saw houses in all stages of development, from foundation to naked beams and brick and shingle sidings. Lumber, bricks, plumbing supplies strewn over the landscape. The two story building called The Women's Reproductive Services had tall grass against the side of the building. Behind the building was an old railway spur, where in times past a train may have dropped off a boxcar.

In front of the building there were women. It appeared to Asa that there may have been twenty or thirty women of all sizes, shapes and colors. Some of the women were obviously pregnant. On the side farthest away from him, near the shoreline of the lake were children. It reminded Asa of maybe the children in a Day Care Center. They seemed to be different sizes. *I've really need to get glasses. I know there are children, some maybe even teenagers, but at this distance all I see is shapes.* "Tom, look over there near the shore line?"

Looking up and in the direction Asa was pointing, "Yeah, so?" answered Tom. "Doesn't that look like a bunch of kids?"

"Yeah, Asa it does. I need to get closer. That is if I can get past the barricades."

"Asa! Look behind you?"

Wiping his eyes, and turning, "What?" Questioned Asa.

"Those two standing back there." Pointing, "That tall Indian. Isn't he Tribal Police?" Probed Tom.

Motioning for Tom to follow, Asa headed for the two Tribal Policemen. "Hey Sam isn't it?"

Looking away from the crowd Sam glanced over and then turned to face Asa, "You are the FBI. I didn't know you were involved in this one."

"What do you mean? We're still looking for our little girl, Jackie Gallagher."

Bending down and scuffing his boot on the gravel, "I got a message." Raising his wild eyebrows, "About the little girl, plus there is information that there are two missing teenagers that are here."

The two Tribal Policemen, and the two Special Agents started walking to the roped off areas where they spotted children. Agent Tom Walton was about six paces in front of the others. Robert literally skips to catch up with him, "Agent Walton."

Slowing down and turning to face, Ride The Horse, "What is it officer?"

"Well Sam and me checked with the Sheriff of Lake County, we were sent to the Waukegan Police Station, and after all that Sam and me were told we could not get a warrant cause we didn't have Probable Cause. So how are we going to get a look at those kids?"

"Well Robert. It is Robert right?"

"Yes. I'm the guy that screwed up, by letting someone take that little girl off the Rez."

"Well Robert I expect that someone gave you a good talk. And just remember this the federal government trumps state, county, and city. Plus we do have Probable Cause. We traced an IP address to this very location."

Several uniformed police officers came up to the group of four, "Sorry you can't go beyond the barricade."

Asa didn't a say a word, he just pulled out his badge, and ID. The police at the barricade lifted the yellow tape.

Walking over to the children, and surveying the unusually subdued group of children. They didn't see anyone that they could recognize, but Sam turned to the others, "Have you ever seen a group of kids so quiet? I know they are supposed to be sick, but there is something not quite right about this."

Asa walking over to the group of kids, turned to face the group of four, "I raised three kids, and even when they were supposed to be sick it was all my wife and I could do to keep them quiet. I'm not saying that there are times when the illness will knock them out, but there are at least a dozen kids here, and they remind me of zombies."

Bending over with his hands on his knees, between gasp for air, Asa turns to Tom and asked, "What do they have here? The sign says Women's reproductive services. Are these kids in some kind of Day Care; you know maybe where a mother can leave her kid while she sees a doctor?"

"You alright Asa?"

After taking a deep breath, Asa answered, "Yeah, just a little winded."

"These kids have been medicated. No five year-old is that spaced." Actually walking in front of each child, and looking, "Asa, I don't see our little girl here. How are Sam and Robert doing?"

Sam seeing Tom coming over, "I don't see our teenagers. We need to get inside that building."

Asa catching up to Tom, "I agree. Hey boys, looks like we have a welcoming committee." Pointing to the large black man, dressed in dark slacks, a turtleneck sweater and a watch cap and a tall skinny blond man in whites. "I don't think they will be very pleased with us." While trying to catch his breath exclaimed Asa.

Walking up the two white colored cement steps, and Asa displaying his badge, the large black man seemed to growl, and the blond orderly stepped aside.

Still struggling for breath, Asa motioned for the Robert, Sam and Tom to come close. "Hand me your cell phones."

Tom just handed his to Asa the two Indians glanced at Asa with confusion.

"We don't have hand-held radios; I know we should have." Taking the cell phones of Robert and Sam, scanning and putting his number in the phone. "Now just keep that on speaker; I should be able to talk with you and you with me. I've called our local office, and they are sending back-up, but in the meantime we need to tear this place apart before they have a chance to move the girls."

Tom opened double doors and found himself staring at a receptionist behind a counter. Looking directly and the heavyset woman in a nurses uniform, "Why aren't you outside with everyone else?"

Looking up at Asa with a belligerent look on her face, and a very annoying nasal sounding voice, "I knew it was a false alarm. I didn't see smoke or anything and I just haven't got time to waste on these games."

"OK, just stay where you are, and I mean stay in that chair. You and I are going to have a little talk." Pointing to the metal door behind the receptionist, "What is behind that door?" Demanded Asa. Putting his wireless to his mouth, "Can everybody hear me?"

There was three responses, "I need one of you guys up front. I think I need to baby sit."

"I've checked most of the offices on the second floor and utility rooms. It seems pretty quiet. I will have to get back up here Give me two minutes and I'll be there." Replied Robert.

Asa, was starting to sweat. He moved to one of the stuffed chairs near the receptionist. Putting his hand up to his chest, then digging into his back pocket, pulling out a handkerchief and wiping his brow.

Just as Robert arrived in reception he heard the sound of cars in front, glancing out the glassed doors he could see a dark colored SUV, and several dark blue sedans. Looking over at Asa, "I think the Calvary has arrived." Then staring at Asa, "You're not looking so good. Are you alright?"

Taking a deep breath and then sliding off the chair. Robert came running over as the receptionist grabbed a sweater that was on the back of her chair, and casually walked out the same doors that the agents were entering. Robert ran to his partner and put a finger on

Asa's carotid artery, then on his wrist. Looking up just as Sam entered the room, "Sam, Agent Williams is dead."

A uniformed police officer entered followed by FBI Special Agents. Sam held his hand up, and asked, "Are there EMTs out there?"

Sam! Did you see where the receptionist went? I saw her just before Asa dropped."

The police officer shook his head, "Yes sir." He turned and opening the doors, and called, "We need EMTs in here."

The EMTs put a sheet over Asa and lifted him onto a gurney, raised the gurney and wheeled him out.

Special Agent Tom Walton found himself in a large room with an oven in the center. There was a door on the far side of the room. He approached the door and when he opened it his stomach felt as if it dropped. What he saw was a room with at least a dozen teenagers lying in beds on yellow soiled sheets. The girls appeared to be drugged. He heard what sounded like the croak of a frog. Then it sounded like words, "Mister, Mister, please."

The girls in the beds all seemed to be unconscious except for one. Tom found the teenager with an IV in her arm. Touching her head, "What's your name child?"

Looking up through eyes so swollen that they were barely slits, "Where is Ellen?"

"Who are you?" Sam probed.

Barely above a whisper, "I'm Sarah. Where's Ellen?"

Holding her face in his hands, "Sarah, I'll be right back, and I promise we will find Ellen." Arriving in the reception area, going over to a pale Asa, lying on the floor and scrutinizing the reception area. "Something is wrong." Observing Sam and Robert. Sam walking over to Tom, putting his hand on Tom's shoulder, "Asa is gone." Looking up at Sam, "Where did he go? No he just past out"

"Tom… Asa is dead."

"How?"

"Pretty sure it was a heart attack."

Several more police officers came into the reception area. "OK, we need help. I've got a warrant here and we need to go through this building looking over every inch." Instructed Tom.

"Your right we need to get back to our search. By the way has anyone seen this illusive Doctor?" Remarked Sam.

"Sam, will you come with me? I think I found one of your teenagers, or at least one of them."

Not much bothered Sam. He was able to tolerate many different smells such as rotted vegetation, the carcasses of decaying animals, but the putrid smell of human waste and regurgitation. Perusing young girls, barely in their teens laying in their own waste. Then he saw her. He pulled a photo of a teenaged girl out of his shirt pocket. "Yes Tom that is one of the girls I'm looking for."

"Why are you looking so down? You found one of the girls."

"Yeah, but I still need to find the other one, plus the other reason I left Big Sky country. I really thought we would have little Jackie. And of course, your partner. I really didn't know him, but I think he would have been accepted even among **my** people."

"You know Asa was a Jew, and he used to joke that he was part of the missing tribe of the Israelites. So maybe he really was one of your brothers."

There were women wandering around the entrance when Tom asked one of the police officers, "Tell those women that this clinic is closed."

Several of the women tried pushing past the barricades and the police officers. Tom overheard some say, "What are we supposed to do?" Another said, where can we go now?"

Most of the uniforms had departed. There were four patrol officers watching the doors. Tom called Sam and Robert to come close. "Robert did you finish your search?"

"No Asa called and said he needed help. I checked most of the offices, and a couple of broom closets upstairs, but there is a whole area that I haven't looked at yet."

"OK. Why don't you and Sam finish up together? I'll have the agents from the Chicago office help me with my report. Where is Asa when I need him? He was always so much better at making my reports understandable."

Robert was heading for the stairwell, he turned and looked at Tom. "I know we found Sarah, but we are still missing a teenager and little Jackie."

Sam started to walk with Robert toward the stairwell, "You know I found Sarah and several other women in an open ward just beyond the operating room. I bet there are kids here too."

Stopping in front of one of the Agents from the Chicago office, Tom requested "Arrange for transportation to a hospital for these women. If I'm not mistaken there will be children to transport. I just don't know how many."

"I need to get back upstairs. I was just about to check the end of the hallway when Asa called. That could be where we will find the little Gallagher girl." Declared Robert.

On the second floor Robert noticed double doors to his right. He opened the doors and found himself in a dining hall. There was a serving area; stainless steel steam table, a commercial oven and on one side of the oven was a grill and the other side was a four burner stove. He saw the walk-in cooler. Opening the door he saw shelves with wide mouthed thermos bottles. On the floor was a large stainless tub with potatoes in it. In the back of the walk-in was what looked like a freezer door? Inside the freezer there was frozen vegetables, and large slabs of frozen beef on the shelves.

Coming out of the food service area by a single door in the rear of the kitchen, Robert heard sounds. It sounded like puppies or maybe kittens. He open the last door in the hallway. What he observed were small beds used as cribs, and several toddler beds. There were small children in all, but one of the toddler beds. There were three metal cribs two had babies in them.

Pulling out his wireless phone, Robert request, "This is Robert. Can you hear me?"

"Yeah Robert I hear you. What do you need?"

"I found kids. Small, young kids, a couple of babies. I need medical assistance to transport these kids."

"10-4."

Sam opened a door on the far side of a room that looked like an operating room, with a stainless steel examining table, what was probably an operating bed. There was an assortment of scalpels, and a pair of scissors on a stainless steel table. He opened the door on the far side of the room. What he saw was the stocky mousy haired woman, the same woman that he saw at Crow Agency. She was sitting in an old wooden rocking chair with a fully formed fetus, in her lap with its legs kicking. He couldn't help but stare at the child. It looked as if the child should be crying, except its skull was crushed. There was gray mater puddled around the woman's feet. She had tears running down her cheeks, and she was staring at the wall, rocking back and forth, and moaning.

He finally recovered enough to look around the room. Next to the woman was a shallow ceramic tub. Next to the tub was a deep stainless sink. In the wall were large drawers. The drawers were the kind Sam had seen in the medical examiners lab. Sam went over to the drawers and started pulling them open.

The first drawer Sam opened had the body of a girl, possibly 15-years-old. She was covered in a blue gown, her black hair was matted against her forehead. She was African American. He pushed the drawer back and opened the drawer near the bottom. For some reason he knew this was what he would find. He reached in his shirt pocket and pulled out the photo. This was definitely Ellen. The gown she was wearing was bloodied. There was blood that had spread out under her, the blood was now coagulated.

Standing straight and backing away from the drawer, Sam pulled out his wireless phone, "Tom, when the paramedics come send them back here. You might want to get the medical examiner back here too.

The sun was glaring through the bedroom blinds as Russell was attempting to pull himself out of bed. His toes and fingers were a grayish blue and felt very cold and painful, his feet were cold and his toes numb, as were his fingers. *How can my feet hurt and feel numb at the same time?*

Trying to yell, but with little luck. Speaking as loud as he could, "Naomi, could you come in here?"

Just then the phone rang. With some effort he did manage to lift the receiver, "Hello."

"Russ, this is Cyrus. I think you might like this."

"Don't keep me on suspense."

"Boy these Feds really take their cyber forensics seriously."

"Get to the point."

"Well at about 0-dark-thirty we finally got a trace on that address."

"Come on Cy, get to the point."

Sounding exasperated, Cyrus replied. "Sorry chief. The FBI team took their Gulf Stream out and headed for Chicago. This may be the news you have been waiting for."

Shaking his hands, then rubbing them together, Russ switch the phone receiver from one ear to the other, "Listen Cyrus, I'm sorry. I didn't mean to sound like a real son-of-a-bitch. It's just that I woke with the grand-mother of all aches."

"I understand. I ain't got kids. I have no idea of what you afre going through. I really would like to hear what you guys came up and how you did it."

"Hey Russ, if you and Naomi are up to it, Sal and I would like to take you guys out to breakfast."

With a sigh, "Cyrus, it sounds great, but I don't know where we will find a babysitter in this short notice,"

"Just get Naomi, and the kids dressed; normal Saturday digs. In other words out of the PJs. We'll be over in about an hour."

Sitting at a locale Denny's the Gallagher's were drinking coffee with the Grangers the boys where finishing up their pancakes. Anthony was exceptionally quiet; it was as if he were a thousand miles away. Oh he contributed to the conversations only if someone directed the conversation towards him.

Naomi reached across the table and placed the back of her hand on Anthony's forehead. Looking over at Russ, "he doesn't seem to be running a fever. By the way how are you doing?"

Closing his hands and making fists, "Whatever it was I think it is getting better." Russell eyeballed Cyrus, "OK, buddy you were all excited when you called this morning.

What did you find out?"

Both women were quiet. Cyrus looked over at Russ, "First it looks like the little Middle Eastern doctor mess up. He may be smart. The cyber forensic lad is awesome." Russ was looking impatient. "When we left your house the other night we had an idea where your little girls might be, but Doctor Abide was getting greedy. He advertised on the internet, and according to the cyber guys, he left a finger print."

Naomi with tears welling up in her eyes, implored Cyrus, "Please don't do this. Tell us what you found out."

Rubbing his crew-cut Cyrus was trying not to act too excited, "The good news is…" Naomi interjected, "Good news! That means that there is bad news."

"As I was saying Agent Williams and Agent Walton took the FBI gulf Stream as soon as we found out the physical address of the computer that was used to broadcast your baby's picture. They found a facility where they were holding women and children. Tom Walton said that he knows Jacki was there. They rescues a lot of women and children."

Russ looked over at Cyrus, "But not Jackie."

With his face getting red, "No Russ. Not yet, but it is a matter of time."

Naomi almost to the point of breaking down, "I'm sorry Cyrus, but we have been hearing that for weeks now."

"I haven't heard from Asa or Tom since they left. I thought for sure that Agent Williams would at least contact you. They should be checking- in. As a matter of fact they should have checked-in hours ago. The people at the bureau assured me they would call. Bureau…is that short for Bureaucracy; oh that's right. I thought that the Air Force had their cookie cutters and dealing in Red Tape was a military thing."

Naomi and Russell were just staring at Cyrus. Both boys looked first at Cyrus and them their parents.

"Sorry. I didn't mean to start raving. Let me give them a call. Maybe they tried to call." The expression on Cyrus Granger's face went from a deep red to a very sallow yellow. "What is it? Did they find our daughter? What's wrong?" Implored Russ.

With a breath and a sigh, Cyrus stated, with a catch in his throat, "The good news is Jackie wasn't there."

"That's the **good** news? What the hell is the bad news?

In a monotone, Cyrus stated, "They are sure she was there, but somehow she slipped out while the facility where they were holding her. There was child in the same room with Jackie. She had been playing like she was asleep when she saw a little boy. It seems this boy was white. She said, not just white but like a white powder, with very pale blue eyes. The little boy pulled the needles out of the little girl's arms and untied her. Evidently he came back an untied that child."

With tears in her eyes, Naomi looked up at Cyrus. "OK. What about my little?"

Cyrus said, "I am only relaying what I heard on the phone just seconds ago. After the alarm went off one of the agents went in the building, found the room, which just had empty beds. According to Agent Walton, it appeared that Jackie had left the hospital gown on the bed and changed into her clothes. The child that was talking to Agent Walton, said that the white boy half carried half dragged the little girl."

Putting his hands behind his neck, Russ, commented, "OK. If that is the good news what's the bad news?"

"Agent Asa Williams is dead. Tom and the two Tribal Policemen are searching for Jackie as we speak. Seems they are looking for this little very pale white boy as well." Cyrus said as he looked over at Anthony. Sam, one of the tribal policemen called the little boy "The Ghost that walks."

Russell stared at his son. Then shook his head. Barely audible, "No! That is impossible." Naomi glanced at Russ, "What did you say?"

Now rubbing the back of his neck, "Sorry. I am having a hard time taking this all in." Naomi staring at Cyrus, then back down at her coffee. She appeared to be getting anxious. "We have to do something. I just can't sit here and wait. It seems like we have been waiting for months."

"Let's go back to the house. We can wait there as well as anyplace else." Proposed Russell.

Naomi looked over at Sally, "Why don't you guys come over the house?"

Sally looked over at her husband, and then at Russ and Naomi, "We'd like that, but how about we come over a little later this afternoon. There are a few things we need to do." Sally peering at Naomi over her coffee cup, "Naomi I can't know what you're going through. I don't know what to do. We've just met. I'm not sure if I should leave you alone are be with you?"

Denny was just staring at his parents. Anthony seemed to be staring into space.

"I appreciate that Sally, but I think Russ and I need a little alone time. Plus I don't know what is going on with Anthony. Maybe he didn't get his sleep out. He doesn't seem to be running a fever. Just a little nap should help him."

Chapter 19

Leaning against the door frame to what appeared to be a pathology lab, the heavy woman with the mousy hair was still sitting in a rocking chair rocking back and forth, and making moaning sounds. It was obvious to Sam that this woman was strung out n something. Sam had seen and even known people on the Rez that were strung out mostly on alcohol, but he had seen his share of the few that got carried away with peyote, even a few that used pharmaceuticals, but most of them looked skinny, anemic, sickly with bleeding gums. He'd seen this woman before.

Darlene was staring into space. She couldn't think of a thing but the scream of the baby as that man squished its skull. Where is Melvin, she started thinking, then she felt sounds coming out of her. All she could utter, was, "Melvin...Melvin."

Two large muscular men wearing white arrived at the pathology lab. Sam just pointed to the woman in the rocking chair. One of the men in white looked down into the woman's lap, turned toward the ceramic tub and throw-up. The other man turned to Sam just as Special Agent Tom Walton walked in. "You want her or what?" Exclaimed one of the men in white.

"Can you take her to the State Mental Health Hospital?" Asked Tom.

The man that throw-up was still leaning over the ceramic tub. The one by the door replied, "She'll be over at Aurora. I've got some paperwork for you to sign."

When Sam and Tom came back to the reception area, Robert was talking to what appeared to be a girl of twelve, possibly thirteen. Motioning for Tom, "This girl says that she saw the doctor leave with a big man. It looked as if they were in a hurry."

Tom put his hand out to the girl; she backed away. He immediately backed away. "Sorry. What's your name?"

With a shaky voice and sounding as if she were about to cry. "I'm Susann."

"Susann, did you see a little redheaded three-year-old?"

"Yes sir."

"Do you know where she went?"

"Yes sir. A little white boy took the needles out of her arms and unfasted the straps that were holding her in the bed. He took her out of the room. I was supposed to be asleep but I was just playen possum. I tried call to him, but my throat hurt and I had redouble yelling. He mist of heard me cause he came back and told me to get the other kids out of there. Then he ran with the little girl. He was half carrying her and half dragging. Told me to hurry."

"Do you know where they went?"

"No, but." Pointing to a tall girl with blond curly hair, "That girl was my babysitter her name is Sandy, the white boy got her out too. She told one of the other agents where she saw the doctor go. I don't know what happen to the little girl and the white boy."

Just then one of the agents from the Chicago office came over to Tom, "You have to be Tom Walton from Baton Rouge."

Tom looked up and a tall skinny pock marked man with thing black hair, "You got me."

"I'm Don Wilson, out of the Chicago. I hope you don't mind, but when they carried Agent Williams out of here I called it in to the office. I also told the office about what we found here. Told them they would get a written report as soon as I could get to it. I am really sorry about your partner."

"Thanks. I wasn't really thinking about writing reports."

The few uniformed police officer were interviewing the people remaining in or near the Women's Reproductive Services. The children were being gathered by representatives from the Cook County Child Protective Services. Names and Addresses of the women remaining were reluctantly supplied by the few women that remained.

Sitting on a pier watching the commotion around a large freighter, Melvin is gazing at the cargo being lifted into the cargo hold. "Larry, what are we doing here? Don't you think we should be putting distance away from that clinic?"

Pacing back and forth, Al-abadi stops and turns to face Melvin, "Relax my friend. We will both be on our way, and far from this place. Just as soon as they finish loading that ship."

Running his hands through his thick then pulling his hair back, and securing his hair in a ponytail using a thick rubber band, "Larry, we are standing out just sitting here watching a big ship Loading cargo."

"You are right, Melvin. Let me find the Captain. He knows me and there is a place for us on his ship."

Pushing himself up, "Than what? What happens when we go aboard? Where are we going?"

Motioning for Melvin to follow, Al-abadi, "I see the Captain. For you information we will go through the St. Lawrence Seaway the out into the Atlantic. We will be in Damascus shortly."

"Larry I need to know, what happened to Darlene? She went in to help you and I haven't seen her. Where is she? She may not be much to you but she has been my woman for a long time."

"Your woman is damaged. She is of no further use to either one of us."

Melvin started to say something just as a dark bearded man approached. Al-abadi spoke at length. Tuning to Melvin and motioning for him to follow, "Come we must hurry."

"I will not leave until you tell me what happened to Darlene."

Both Al-abadi, and Melvin turned at the sound of cars and sirens at the end of the pier. The man that Al-abadi called Captain was at the top of a large gangway motioning for the crane to pull the gangway up.

The small dark Middle Eastern doctor was casually moving toward the dock workers. Melvin looked over toward Al-abadi, just as a uniformed policeman grabbed his arms and cuffed him.

Tom Walton and Robert Ride The Horse arrived just in time to see Melvin being placed in a patrol car.

Robert turned to Tom, and questioned, "Is that it? Where is the Doctor, the little Arab.?"

"I know you don't want to hear this, but I think he got away by blending in with the doc hands." I bet you've heard this before..."

"Hear what?"

"That they all look alike."

Robert just tightened his jaw and stared at Tom, then with the start of a smile and sowing his white teeth, that is what we say about whites."

༄

Sitting on a cushioned bench to the right of the reception desk at the Women's Reproductive Services, with his gray sweat stained Stetson on his knees Sam was just cradling his head in his large hands. He heard a sound. It sounded like a young boy. He felt something tugging at his leg. Looking up he saw Anthony.

Shaking Sam's leg, Anthony with his arm around a very little redheaded girl, "Mr. Whitehorse would you please take my sister home. I am not sure they are at home. We live in St. Petersburg."

Rubbing is red watery eyes, Sam looked over at Anthony, "Why can't you take her home?"

I don't know, I tried when I first found her, but couldn't do it."

"Yes Anthony I will take your sister home. Will you be there?"

"Yes Mr. Whitehorse I will be there. You will like my dad... Mom too."

༄

Denny was in the back yard. Naomi thought that Anthony needed a nap. There wasn't a sound from the bedroom. Cyrus and Russell were sitting und a shade tree watching Denny When the house phone. Naomi almost tripped over Sally trying to get to the phone.

Out of breath and dropping the receiver, "Hello, this is Mrs. Gallagher." She dropped the receiver just as Russ came in the kitchen door.

Grabbing Naomi, Russell questioned with concern, "What is it." Russell, Cyrus, Sally, Jackie is coming home."

At the top of his lungs, Russell yelled, "Denny come in please."

Within seconds a caravan of a maroon Caprice, and a green Jeep Wagoner heading for the Gandy Bridge and to Tampa International Airport.

Sitting in the Tampa Terminal Naomi was the first to see Zack Taylor walk the arrival area. With big brown eyes and the look of someone very pleased. "I just got the word."

Pacing back and forth and staring at the arrival board, trying to make the time go by.

Wishing, and hoping for the announcement that the flight from Chicago has arrived.

Looking at the tunnel from the tarmac Naomi remarked, "Someone bought new" clothes for our baby."

Jumping out of Sam's large hands, Jackie screamed, "Mommy!"

Holding Jackie in her arms and looking at a large Indian. "You must be Sam. Jack warned me that you would be with her."

Sam looked up at the Gallagher's, "She will need to me examine by a doctor." Zackery walked up to the group. "Naomi, Russ it will only take a few minutes, but we have a doctor on stand-by."

THE END

www.ingramcontent.com/pod-product-compliance
Lightning Source LLC
Chambersburg PA
CBHW070548100726
47907CB00004B/1310